Red Hot Lipstick

By the Same Author

Bitter Blue
Black Sugar: Gay, Lesbian and Heterosexual
    Love Poems
Chasing Black Rainbows: A Novel Based on
    the Life of Artaud
Delirium: An Interpretation of Arthur
    Rimbaud
Diamond Nebula
Inhabiting Shadows
Isidore: A Fictional Re-creation of the Life
    of Lautréamont
Lipstick, Sex and Poetry: An Autobiographical
    Exploration of Sexuality
Madness – The Price of Poetry
When the Whip Comes Down: A Novel
    About De Sade

Jeremy Reed

Red Hot Lipstick

Erotic Stories

Peter Owen

London & Chester Springs

PETER OWEN PUBLISHERS
73 Kenway Road London SW5 0RE
Peter Owen books are distributed in the USA by
Dufour Editions Inc. Chester Springs PA 19425-0007

First published in Great Britain 1996
© Jeremy Reed 1996

Acknowledgements go to Erotic Stories *and* For Women,
where some of these stories first appeared.

All Rights Reserved.
No part of this publication may be reproduced in any form or by any means without the written permission of the publishers

A catalogue record for this book is available from the British Library

ISBN 0-7206-0943-7

Printed in Great Britain by Biddles of Guildford and King's Lynn

For John and Denise

So I said, 'But I'll do it. Let's do all the things we ever wanted to do or have done to us. We have the whole night. There are so many objects here that we can use. You have costumes too. I'll dress up for you.'

'Oh, will you?' said Marcel. 'I'll do anything you want, anything you ask me to do.'

Anaïs Nin
Delta of Venus

It is only by admitting night physically that one succeeds in doing away with it morally.

Lautréamont

Contents

The Slave	9
Lauris's Stockings	17
Red Hot Lipstick	23
Devil's Paradise	33
A Boa Constrictor Tamed by a Flower	43
Alice through the Looking Glass	49
Surf and Sensuality	57
Blue by You	63
Flying Kites	71
Blue Bra Straps in a Bookstore	77
Lima Blues	85
Lana's Adventure	93
Catching Stars	103
Tainted Love	113
He Was a She	121
Hunt the Sequin	129
Blues to Eat Your Heart Out	137

The Slave

Jim had always wanted to write about the bizarre sexual fetishes he had cultivated since childhood, but there was somehow a screen dividing experience from words; he could remember the act, but it dipped out of focus when he attempted to put it into language. For a long time he walked across the city carrying his problem uppermost in consciousness. And sometimes he walked out at night when it was raining, greatcoat collar turned up in his blond hair, his footsteps taking him to the river with its slow traffic of litter, dead dreams and huge coiling currents snaking beneath the surface like lianas. He was solitary because he couldn't get it right. He could free-associate and recount anecdotes for friends, but he couldn't get it to come out fluently on the page.

Most of his young life he had worked as a gigolo, he had given his body to men and women and his androgynous sexuality was an integral part of him. It was easy for him; he'd never put up gender barriers and regarded himself as male orientated towards female, or male attracted to male. He liked both and considered it perfectly natural to have this bipolar attraction.

Jim sat on a bench by the Embankment. He took out a red-covered notebook from his pocket. It was already blotched, with a worked-up texture of inclusions and omissions, so that the pages looked like ink drawings rather than writings. He liked to scramble words on the page, and one thought crashed so disconnectedly to the next one that often there wasn't time to link them, and he just wanted to get the whole lot down rather than isolate and select how one perception identified with another. He was speedy and restless, and he hoped writing would slow down his manic rhythm. He watched the water, but it was travelling fast in glaucous runs; a barge went downriver with the tide, leaving a grooved furrow in its wake. He had time, but the words didn't; they always came at him with speed.

He remembered that the day before yesterday he had been called by an elderly Italian countess, and had gone over to the hotel suite in Mayfair where she was waiting for him in a leopard-skin catsuit and black spike heels. She had worn a black face veil to hide her age, and was heavily made up with impasto strokes of foundation. Her front teeth were gold. She had wanted first of all to give him head, and his expansive member had fitted between her gold teeth, as she cat-licked him to excitement. In his mind he had pretended it was a leopard which was sucking him off, and the surreal concept had made him hard. He had run his hands all over her leopard-skin body, searching for a tail at the join between her crotch and bottom. And that thought had really excited him. He had resisted coming, for he knew the countess would wish to be ridden long and hard and he feared he might not regain his enthusiasm so easily if he saw her out of her catsuit. And to his delight the suit was held together across the crotch by three fastenings, and when they were teasingly released he was able to enter her as a leopard. He had enjoyed himself playing with this Italian cat, and her prolonged purrs beneath his undulating body had told him that he was giving fulfilment. She had even bitten him on the shoulder to express her felinity.

Jim had known so many encounters. There was the man he visited who liked to dress up like Marilyn Monroe in a blond wig, floating white dress, and wear a lipstick gash which was the red of a strawberry crushed into a white sheet. This man wanted to be elaborately courted. A dinner table would be prepared with champagne and candles, and his black servant would wait at table, supplying every form of delicacy. Jim had to act out the role of starstruck suitor. He would play footsie with the transvestite beauty, she at first acting coyly towards his tentative advances, and by degrees progressing to the encouragement whereby he would slip off one of her stilettos and she would place a stockinged foot in his lap. This was all to be done circumspectly and under the pretence that the servant had no notion of what was going on under the table. The ritual also demanded that Jim stroke Marilyn's legs, again with surreptitious, fugitive gestures; he made an occasional ladder in her glass nylons to add to his subject's pleasure. And orgasm was achieved by this slow ritual of advances made over a dinner that lasted up to three hours. No other services were demanded of Jim. The evening culminated with his hand slid up Marilyn's skirt; it stayed there until orgasm had been achieved.

He could remember so many other clients who entertained extravagant needs. There was the woman who insisted on being dusted with long plumed feathers. Tied to the bed, and dressed, according to some obsessive fetish, in nothing but army boots, he performed his task, which was to flick feathers over her nipples and pussy. The woman would build by stages to ecstatic orgasm. One day she had asked Jim to coat her body in honey; he had done this with the pot and paintbrush she had supplied, and then he had placed exotic feathers in the viscous sheen on her skin. She had looked like a tropical macaw, and that time she had reached orgasm just like that, her voice imitating bird-song as she rippled convulsively in spasms across the bed.

Jim got some of this down. He looked at the river and attempted to give his words the water's directional fluency. There was no reversing its course, the current headed inexorably downstream. He must do the same. He tried to envisage the process as holding a mirror to his thoughts, and by examining each image as it appeared in a reflective surface, he was better able to slow his stream of consciousness. He began to enjoy the process of writing, rather than suffer frustration at the opposing speed of thought and language. And the whole city looked better as a consequence. Even the fissured, superannuated

South Bank complex opposite took light and appeared to be a meaningful fixture in his personal landscape of the city.

Sunlight was breaking over the river; it lay in white stripes on the water's green coat, and was a sort of sign to Jim that he was getting there. Writing was such a difficult process, but he was beginning to find a way to unlock his memories. He wanted to write a book of sexual memoirs which would be both poetic as well as scandalous in its revelations. He thought about it a long time, not forgetting that he had a client that afternoon, or that the woman had provided no specifics other than that she wanted to be a slave. He was used to bondage devotees, and expected to find the usual sort of private dungeon that such women kept in their Kensington apartments. He was almost casual about the prospects, and noticed that in his morning's communion with the river he had managed to fill four pages of his notebook with only minimal crossings out. He was no longer treating the page as a work text to be scored by contradictions, but as a surface on to which he projected lucidity. He was pleased with the architecture he had imposed on mental chaos. A little bit of his life had been re-experienced, and it was like erecting a building block on the page. If it continued like this he would find the means to write his book. He would end up going back to places he had forgotten and reliving experiences he had thought buried in nervous substrata. Jim was pleased with himself. He hoped the method would continue into the night after the afternoon visit he would pay his client.

When he arrived at the woman's flat, situated off Kensington High Street, he was elated, and his client was unusually pretty: tall, with a luxurious density of black hair, green eyes and the sort of figure owned to by catwalk models. He expressed no surprise that she should contact a gigolo, for experience had taught him that many people were too embarrassed to relate their sexual fantasies to their partner. Their needs often remained like a shipwreck inside the psyche. Jim knew instantly that this was the case with Dolores, as she called herself, and that she was doubtless happily married, and probably lived out an obligatory but unimaginative sex life with her husband.

Jim sat down on the deep red sofa, and Dolores, dressed in a very short skirt, sat down in a blue armchair opposite. Jim was totally relaxed, and he waited patiently for her confession as a prelude to her particular fetish. And he had listened to so many confessions. Women and men placed him in the role of sexual therapist, and he in turn assimilated their most intimate confidences. And in a perverse way he would come to recycle the disclosures given him and convert them into fictions.

'I'll be direct,' she said. 'It's not that my husband's not interested in sex, it's more that he's strait-jacketed by convention. It's like he doesn't have an imagination. If I told him what I wanted he would run out into the street proclaiming my indecency.'

Jim smiled. 'And what is it you want?' he asked. 'You can't shock me. Nobody ever has, and besides I've seen everything and done the lot. I'm fluent with both sexes.'

'I'm a painter,' said Dolores. 'And my husband never ventures into the studio upstairs. I've constructed something up there for my use. It's a cage. I want you to place me inside, and read out a list of things I've prepared to excite me. I want to be a captive, a woman who temporarily belongs to a submissive harem. And when I'm fully excited I want you to enter the cage and make love to me, again locking the door behind you, so that we're imprisoned during the act.

Much to Jim's excitement, Dolores slipped out of her skirt before leading him upstairs. She was wearing seamed stockings and black suspenders and tiny black silk panties. Jim felt his erection spontaneously trigger as Dolores led him up a flight of stairs to her studio. He noticed how she had frescoed the walls and ceiling, and blue, pink and green implosive whorls had imparted a strong energy field to the spacious area. And there was the cage. It had narrow bars and was draped with a black hanging. There was a purple mattress inside, and what looked like a bird-perch facing an oval mirror.

'Here is your text,' Dolores said. 'And please lock the door after me. It will increase my excitement.'

Jim was amazed at her trust; he could, after all, go off and leave her locked inside the cage for her husband to discover. She hopped in with alacrity, and to his surprise sat on the perch like a bird and looked in the mirror. 'Start reading,' she commanded.

He stood back and watched her sitting squat in her black panties, the divide between her legs moist with desire. He took up her script and read out a series of imperatives.

1   Slip your forefinger into your crack, and repeat after me: 'Lick me until I'm silver, and until in my perversity I imagine I've grown a hard cock.'
2   I know you're a bird. Swing on the perch with your legs wide open. I want you to peck the bars. I shall feed you grapes, and you will polish these on your mound.
3   Say after me, 'I want to be taken from behind in a cage. I want to grip the bars with my red talons while you fuck me.'
4   Say after me, 'I'd like to grapple with an eagle, while my husband looks on. I'd like to feel its claws on my back, and as I pulled out its feathers it would turn into a youth.'
5   Say after me, 'I want to be whipped with my wet panties. I'm your slave. You can take me in any way you like, and I'll still give you more.'
6   Say after me, 'Tie me to this perch, and fill the crack of my bottom with black grapes.'
7   I can feel your excitement increasing. Finger yourself fast, and let me hear you howl when you come.
8   I want you to imagine giraffes mating. Their spots are falling on the ground from passion.
9   Say after me, 'I'm as slippery as a banana skin inside. I want your cock to go so far up it comes back out of my mouth. That way I can be fucked and suck you at the same time.'

10   You need to be punished. I'm coming inside and I won't let you know where I've concealed the key.

Jim was shaking with excitement as he took off his clothes, unlocked the cage door and ducked inside. Dolores went down on all fours, and moved up to the bars and rattled them with her fists. Jim was certain that this incident would take high prominence in his book, and he crawled over to her, with a baguette of an erection. Dolores arched up against the bars as he entered her and thrust deep for the interior. He could feel how she intended this act as a vengeance on her husband. Her repressed passion was volcanic. And in order to lever himself deeper into her, he gripped the bars just above her hands, and listened to her commands to tie her with cord. 'Tie me, I'm your slave!' she pleaded. 'Quick, tie my wrists and my feet.'

Jim withdrew and found the cord lying on the purple mattress. He came back and tied her wrists to the bars, and then secured her ankles. 'Tell me I need to be abused as a slave,' she importuned. 'Do what you want with me.'

Jim slid right back up her and began to work her towards a fast orgasmic crescendo. The bars were rattling furiously as the force of his thrusts drove her up against the metal. He had never heard a woman's voice pitched to such urgency as she contracted in circling spasm after spasm, coming with a ferocity that drained him.

'Now flog me,' Dolores requested. 'Cut me sharply across the bottom.' There was a bullwhip inside the cage, and Jim noticed that Dolores had her gold initials stamped on the handle: DLR. He took it up and flexed the coil, hearing the whistle with which it unleashed itself on the air. He stuck the cage several blows in order to develop a flexible hand, and then laid lash to Dolores, his practised aim leaving a thin red welt on her perfectly proportioned bottom. She had asked him to strike six times, and he spaced each lash to allow her time to recover her breath. She never once complained or cried out, but rather pushed her bottom in the air so that his target was made more vulnerably available. After the sixth stroke he untied her. They were both exhausted.

They went back down to the living room and she poured champagne. It was difficult snapping back to reality, and neither of them was able to switch roles successfully. They had known each other with intensity and under extraordinary circumstances. Jim closed his eyes and she did too. His professional code of detachment prevented him from falling in love with this beautiful woman whose husband was clearly so disinterested in her body that he would never see the red and blue welts he had placed across her buttocks.

'You'll come again to my cage, won't you,' she said. 'What about this time next week. The same arrangement?'

Jim promised to return, and took a bus across London back to the river. His mind was still clear. He wanted to write about the slave. He went and sat within view of the river. The tide had changed, and an architecture of grey marble clouds was roofing the city. But he knew he would write. In his recreation of the afternoon he gave Dolores red hair and the name Genevieve. But the rest of it he got down without too much departure from the facts. He again steadied his thoughts in the reflective surface of the now lazier river. He wrote, and his consciousness of time disappeared, and when hours later he looked up there was a red-haired girl sitting on the bench next to his own. She looked French and could well own to the name Genevieve. Writing is magic, he told himself, as he went over to ask her the time. There wasn't anyone else around, and when he called her Genevieve she laughed. It wasn't her name, but she was lonely and gladly accepted his invitation to walk by the river in search of a café.

Lauris's Stockings

Lauris collected stockings. Perhaps the obsession dated back to the time of her first serious boyfriend, and his eagerness to see her unroll a black silk or nylon cocoon the length of her leg, and have the darker area at the top snap tight under a suspender button. And she too had grown to receive sensual pleasure from the unbunching of the silk concertina as it slipped over her painted toenails, and was slowly, sinuously, almost like a lover's caress, brought to a tautness along her thigh. And then there was the alignment of the seams travelling up from the opaque heelpieces, and the dark crescents of the toepieces through which her nails twinkled scarlet. That act had become a fetish, a ritual she performed in privacy for herself as much as for the trained eye in the crowd who could instantly spot the freer play of a stocking from the comparative immobility of tights in their deader set at the knees and ankles. Her first boyfriend had told her that a stocking breathed on a leg like a ripple traced through still water.

It all came back to Lauris as she unpacked the little parcel Paul had sent her through the post. There were stocking packets wrapped in black and red tissue papers, and Lauris stood by the window overlooking the winter park, experiencing an anticipative thrill at the refinement of Paul's taste, and how he had chosen the most translucent 10-denier stockings with Cuban heels, so that the fabric would be transparently weightless on contact with her skin. Paul differed from Lauris's first boyfriend in that his pleasure came from seeing her take off her stockings, in the particularly stylized manner adopted by fifties

17

film stars like Sophia Loren and Gina Lollobrigida, whereas her earlier boyfriend had preferred the reverse process of her slipping stockings on.

Lauris watched a taxi hunt the avenue, a black amphibian cruising towards town. Some of the plane trees retained a crown of orange leaves, and there were red geraniums splashed in window-boxes all along the opposite terrace of houses which had been converted into spacious apartments. Lauris was unconsciously attracted by the idea that someone was watching her, and had been for a long time, perhaps months or years, as she went through the ritual each day of taking a chair to the window and with one leg lifted to the chair, adjusting first the right and then the left stocking, and in the process pushing her skirt tantalizingly up to her waist. In fact she went through the motions with the idea that a complicitous eye was observing an auto-erotic act.

Lauris was anxious to try on the three different pairs of stockings that Paul had selected – Italian and French designs – and she slipped a hand into the bunched silk, exploring the expanding toepiece, and lightly brushing her cheek with the filmy silk, before placing her right leg on the chair, and with calculated suspense unfastening the stocking from a black suspender strap. She released the stocking tentatively, and with the timed delay of a virtuoso strip-artist practising for a club performance later that night.

It was only after the stocking had bunched at her ankle that she removed her black stiletto, and ran her fingers under her arched foot. For Lauris, this was the moment of erotic excitement. She liked to think it was Paul's fingers mapping out the sensitive nerve-lines in her foot as a prelude to lovemaking. There was something about the stockinged foot which excited her to a point of empathetic identification with a man's sexual fantasies over this point of arousal. Taking the stocking off from the foot was like removing a glove. It was the denouement to a leggy ritual. And when Paul performed this act for her, she would come as the last shiver of silk escaped her toes.

Having inched off her right stocking, and in a state of flushed arousal, she went through the same process with the left, only this time it was slower, and she brought herself to orgasm as the silk came clear of her foot. And now she would begin to acquaint herself with Paul's gift, and she hung the two stockings over the chair-back, and got distracted by two huge plane leaves floating off into the air like mottled stars. And in the time of watching them go, Lauris became aware of someone in the apartment opposite, a figure that seemed to have swum into view like a big fish streaking to the surface of a lake. Suddenly there was black hair, eyes, a nose, lips, and a woman's curvaceous body dressed in a black bra and black panties, black suspenders and black stockings. For a moment Lauris thought she was looking at herself in a mirror, for the woman had also positioned a chair at the window, and with a mirror on the wall behind her, Lauris was able to view her from the front and from behind. She was voluptuously attractive, and the position of one gloved hand between her thighs told Lauris that she was deriving vicarious pleasure from the teasing strip-tease she had made into a daily ritual.

Lauris felt no embarrassment at this voyeuristic union. On the contrary, she experienced a rush of excitement at the knowledge that she was performing to a solitary watcher, someone who might have been observing her stockings fetish for months, and experiencing a mutual pleasure at the conspiratorial pact.

Their eyes had met, and Lauris was determined not to appear self-conscious, or to impart anything to her motions which would in any way indicate that she was exaggerating her pleasure for the sake of her accomplice. But inspired by her observer's state of undress, Lauris unzipped her skirt and let it fall to the floor like an orange flower. She delighted in the fact that she was wearing black silk panties like her neighbour, and a suspender belt of pink and black lace. She felt naturally exhibitionist, and turned her back to her watcher so that the woman could observe the compact roundness of her bottom, the curve of her hips, and the shapely elongation of her thighs. She stood like that for a minute, bringing her hands up behind her head and extracting the two pins from her hair so that the chignon released a luxurious stream of blond hair that tumbled to midback. Lauris felt unprecedentedly confident, as though months of rehearsal were culminating in the expert gestures she was about to perform.

She turned round and faced the chair. She could see that the woman opposite was standing in profile to her chair, waiting to adopt whatever pose Lauris was willing to dictate. And so it began, the easy exchange of rhythms, for the other woman had also bunched her previously taut stockings round her ankles, and was willing to respond to each of Lauris's improvised gestures, as she coerced Paul's gift over her sensitized left leg. Even though her greater thrill came from releasing the stocking, Lauris manifested a feline satisfaction in knowing that the other woman's stocking was similarly travelling over her leg, the cool film warming to the skin like pearls do to the throat. When Lauris looked across she could see the other woman spellbound by the synchronicity of their actions.

She continued, and the idea of Paul stabbed across her consciousness. She set to wondering how he would respond to this situation, and whether his uptake would be one of sexual fascination or jealous repulsion. Lauris found herself overtaken by increasing pleasure, and she could hear a second and a third taxi reconnoitre down below, before cruising the length of the avenue towards town. Somewhere in her mind Lauris entertained the notion that Paul was expected in the middle afternoon, but that was a hazy concept which soon receded under the stimulus of increased sexual excitement.

When Lauris looked over to her neighbour's apartment, she could see that the woman had switched the light on, and the additional clarity afforded by this brought her into even closer focus, and enhanced the detail of the woman's abundant curves. Lauris caressed the second stocking before coaxing it over her foot, and felt sure her provocation would be reciprocated. With the light on, she felt the winter day outside push at the window like a blue tide. Nothing mattered any more but this concentrated act, and her splayed red fingernails drifted to the gusset of her black silk panties, and brushed the moist pressure accumulating there. Her fingertips were light, and she opened herself petal by petal, as though her way led to the centre of a pink rose. She refrained from sitting astride the chair and working herself to ecstasy, but she was coming to that, and would reach it.

Her neighbour too had her head thrown back, and was beginning the stages which would lead to convulsive climax. Her dark hair was clouded to a storm over her shoulders. Both women were building towards an autonomous excitement which would dispense with the need for inhibitions. Lauris had brought her silk stockings down from her suspender straps to her ankles. She had removed her blouse and her black bra, and was dressed in nothing but her suspenders and panties. She could hear a taxi pull up below, the motor idling while the passenger paid the fare, but she felt it was too early for Paul. The car negotiated its way into traffic, and there was a tugging of wind outside in the treetops. Lauris kept on thinking it was all like a film, and that her ritual each day was removed from time. It was part of another reality.

She sat in the chair and opened her legs wide. She didn't need to watch to know that the woman opposite would be copying her position. Lauris was resolved on reaching maximum pleasure, and that potential was heightened by the fantasies she nurtured of her neighbour in the opposite flat. Lauris contracted and the sensations made her scream with tremulous ecstasy. And if not once, then twice, a third and fourth time she built to unrestrained pleasure.

She stayed there for a time, head over the back of the chair, her body in a state of exhausted abandon. When she got up to draw the curtains, she noticed that the other woman had already done so. She was faced by a red-curtained blank. Lauris looked down into the street. There was a man staring up at the house from the pavement on the opposite side. It could have been anyone, but she knew it was Paul. He was wearing the familiar black woollen coat and emerald scarf. He waved up, and she returned his gesture. She knew that within moments the buzzer would ring.

Red Hot Lipstick

Mostly it was at Harvey Nichols. But there were other stores he visited too – Selfridges, Harrods and Fortnum and Mason. His singular interest in these brilliantly lit emporia was the make-up counters. He was fascinated not only by the subtle palettes of eye shadows, the dark blues and blacks of mascaras, and the red tonal vibrancy of lipsticks, but also by the girls who worked on these counters. He entertained the fantasy that he would make love to one of these lightly made-up assistants, and he would demand a different sort of application of make-up in the course of living out his mental obsessions.

It was a Thursday. He always associated Thursday with whiteness and the sea. As a child he had lived in a town where most shops closed on Thursday afternoons, and he associated the particular white glare in the sea sky with dragging a green deckchair down to the lazy surf line, and spending the afternoon there doing nothing but thinking and watching the curved bottoms of girls in minimal bikinis as they sauntered across the beach. He watched for the little white skin marks in those places where the two triangles were particularly close fitting. He liked girls with copper-coloured bodies and white bottoms. It had excited him to think of laying a whip across those untanned buttocks, or leaving a bite on the left-hand cheek which would colour like a mauve tattoo. And he hoped always that their bodies were entirely shaved, for a depilated pubis could also wear the mark of his own distinctive kiss. Why shouldn't a beach girl go home with a love-bite on her pussy?

When he got to Harvey Nichols, his voyeuristic eye having

already caught sight of a flicker of black panties underneath a mini-skirt on the escalator up, he was fired for the hunt. His life as a painter allowed him the freedom to regulate his working hours as he wished. He strolled into the make-up department, and found it agreeably quiet. There was no insistent crush of tourists obscuring the display counters. He had the freedom to move in on the attractive Japanese girl working on the Shiseido counter. She had made up in beiges and ivories, but her lips were a Matisse red.

He began with his usual ritual of looking at lipsticks, but with such an intimate knowing eye that the assistant would assume that the product was intended for him or someone whose features he knew particularly well. He began with Dragon's Fire, that purple lipstick which still contains a red pigment, and with sexual gestures he pointed the colour up, and instead of testing it on the back of his hand, he applied it meticulously to his lips. The traditional reserve of the Japanese girl didn't break. And with expertly textured mauve lips, he looked direct into her eyes and smiled. 'I need a tissue,' he said, 'as I want to try the red called Vermeil.'

She provided him with a tissue, and asked, 'Are you an actor, or a musician?' He had noticed that this was always the way women qualified men who wore make-up. It made them feel instantly better if the man said, 'I'm a ballet dancer or a stage artist.'

'I'm neither,' he said. 'I just find it's such a turn-on to women. When women see men in red lipstick it makes them feel, well, sexy.' The girl laughed shyly as he made a dramatic flourish of removing one colour for the hectic red he was about to apply. He knew that with his white face and high cheekbones, the red would stand out as an attractive flourish.

'Are you a painter?' the girl laughed. 'Your technique seems pretty good.'

'I'm just that,' he said, working the lipstick to a thick base on his lower lip, and drawing the line thinner on the upper, in order to make a pronounced bow. He took a long time, for he wanted the act to be a sort of courtship: as he predicted, the girl was fascinated by the finesse with which he made himself up.

And all the time he was thinking how later tonight he would tickle her pussy. He would run an adept finger over the moist ridge of her thin panties and watch her eyes mist as he inserted it beneath, all the while guiding her fingers with his other hand to the taut bulge beneath his zip. He might even have her place chopsticks either side of his shaft as her small red mouth closed over his head. She would suck him in with the same delicacy she applied to sushi. Little by little he would be engorged by a silk tongue and, impossibly, his huge desire would be accommodated by her elastic mouth.

He was thinking of this all the time that he was trying the red in the mirror she held up for him. She was clearly interested in a man who was willing to display such temerity in public. This simply wouldn't have happened back home.

'Which colour do you prefer me in?' he said. 'It's up to you, as I'll be wearing it for you tonight.' And again he was imagining her pelvic rhythm, and the constriction of her narrow vaginal muscles as he opened her body to pivot on his cock. 'I'd like to kiss a girl like you, in his scarlet one,' he reflected.

She laughed in the nervous way that Japanese girls do, repressing the full emotion and translating it into an embarrassed giggle. But he knew that he had her now. She was too fascinated to resist his advances, and he said, 'I'll buy the red one for our date tonight. I'll give you my card. Please come to dinner at eight. I'll be expecting you. I think you're very pretty, and maybe you'll want to wear the Dragon's Fire for me tonight.'

He could see the girl was marginally confused, but she wasn't going to reject him. 'Do come, I really like you, and would like to meet you outside your place of work.'

'You're very different,' she commented. 'Are you sure you're interested in women? You're not gay?'

'Come and find out,' he smiled, repeating his sincere request for an evening rendezvous.

'OK,' the girl said. 'It's all out of the ordinary, but I'll come at eight.'

He went off with his purchase, not even bothering to remove the lipstick he had applied, got into a taxi in order to avoid hostile scrutiny on the street, and went home. He was already fantasizing about how he would apply lipstick to her slit, and make it up with all the attention given to lips, adding a bow as perfect as any worked into a satin finish by Lana Turner. He would excite this girl with the point of the lipstick, running the tip of it over her clitoris, and listen to her subdued scale of pleasure break slowly into more demonstrative notes. He would use the lipstick as the tiny cosmetic penis which would leave her delirious for his eventual entry. He imagined tickling her anal bud with it, and extending his artistry to the soles of her feet, and the mauve areolas round her nipples.

But chiefly he liked the idea of chopsticks delicately holding his erect penis.

In order to control his sexual excitement, he spent the next few hours painting. He was working on an abstract canvas incorporating mauve and blue forms, and some impulse within him articulated a pair of scarlet lips as central to the composition.

When the girl arrived at exactly eight, he was surprised by the risks she had taken in appearance. Her lips were the pronounced mauve of Dragon's Fire, her face was powdered white, and her eyes were emphasized with black. She wore a mauve silk blouse, a very short black leather mini-skirt and sheer black tights. She was clearly prepared for the unusual nature of her date.

He poured her the whisky she requested, and watched as she arranged her silk legs like two flowers. His eyes rushed over the expanse of her exposed thighs. She was telling him how back home in Tokyo she was an art student, and that she had come to London for the summer break in order to improve her command of English. Knowing so much about the aesthetics of colour, it had seemed a happy option that she should work with Shiseido or Kanebo. She seemed relaxed in his company and without a trace of the formal characteristics which are traditionally a part of Japanese women. She made no self-conscious attempts to adjust the hem of the tiny skirt she was wearing. On the contrary she seemed to delight in the fact that she was an oriental girl dressed in almost nothing. And he could see that her legs were good ones, and that two thin black seams ran down the back of her tights. She asked for a second whisky, and to his excitement he caught sight of a violet triangle as she recrossed her legs. He liked girls who wore mauve panties, and he knew instinctively that soon he would be exploring the intimate contours of her body. He suggested they go upstairs to his studio, so that he could show her some of his recent work. Out of courtesy he allowed her to precede him up the steep flight of stairs, and by following he could gain a partial view up her skirt. His erection triggered. It was hard to restrain himself from reaching out and tickling her as she walked in an unhurried manner up the stairs. She even removed her shoes halfway up, for the latter were unmanageable stilettos, and the intimacy of this act, and the sight of the black heels and toepieces of her stockinged feet, lit him up with sexual heat. He was longing to place his red-lipsticked mouth over her clitoris.

They never even got to the studio. He offered to show her a recent painting which he'd hung in his bedroom, a temporary location before it went to a client. And as she stood there looking at the blue composition, the unthinkable happened. He placed his hands around her from behind, pressed his lips into her neck, drew her bottom over his straining erection, released it momentarily, unzipped her tight skirt which fell to the ground like a crumpled leather flower, and there she was standing in her seamed tights and violet silk panties, his hand slipping between the divide of her legs from the back, and her mouth open suddenly in a passionate O.

He picked her up and carried her to the bed. Her kisses were responsively hot, and her fingers began to travel up and down his spine like a pianist's. He crushed his red lips into her mauve. Their convoluted tangles worked towards immediate lovemaking, but he resisted the rush. He wanted to work on her like a body artist.

He slipped her panties to one ankle, reapplied a generous coating of red lipstick, and began to bruise her pussy with kisses. She let out thin little cries, her breath deepening, her legs going up so that he could advance his kisses. Unknown to her, he had a pair of chopsticks in his pocket as well as an assortment of lipsticks. He wasn't going to let her come yet. He kept holding off as she built towards orgasm. He took a red lipstick from his pocket, and heightening his pleasure by telling her what he was about to do, he used the soft point to outline a red oval round her pussy. He pulled back from his art work to address it objectively. It was just the stimulus he needed. Only he might change it to pink or orange. Or to mulberry or crimson or mauve. And now he advanced his game, all the time enticing her with his whispered motives. He ran the soft point of the lipstick over her swollen clitoris. He did it so gently that she gasped. And then he repeated the gesture, asserting a light and then firmer pressure, as though he really was working on a painting. Her body responses told him precisely how much she was enjoying the experience. She kept wanting to be taken to orgasm, but he held back. He tickled her mercilessly with the red lipstick tongue, and the bizarreness of the action drove her crazy. Her endearments were mounting to discreet obscenities, and then overt ones. She was desperate for his cock, but he would give her no more than the lipstick. And in turn he described its red action on her clit.

'I'll enter you,' he whispered, 'after you've done something very special for me. Please don't laugh at my request. It's a fantasy I need to live out. I want you to take my erection between these chopsticks, and nibble my cock as though you're eating sushi. I want you to take it in by deepening degrees until you're deep-throating me. And I want you to dab your purple lipstick all over my length.'

He sat up, back to the three deep pillows, in order to watch her crawl between his legs with the chopsticks, her tongue protruding between her purple lips. She flicked it like a snake does as it closes on its prey. At first she just darted the point of her tongue against his head, rather in the tantalizing way he had directed the lipstick at her clitoris. She didn't want to make him come until he had entered her properly. Then she would twist the laval semen out of him in incandescent jabs. She kneaded her lips into his cock, and he stared fascinated by the mauve lipstick blotches she was dispensing across his quivering erection. He was so hard it was like a marble fist. She tormented him with her peppery kisses. She could find all the sensitive spots that only his fingers could meet in solitude, never his lips. And he had longed to be able to place the red dahlia of his own mouth over his penis. She could find every centimetre of his responsive flesh. And all the time he was thinking of how he had painted exactly this scene, a young man in red lipstick reclining against black silk cushions while a Japanese girl, naked on all fours, a pair of chopsticks in one hand, applied head with a purple lipstick. He knew he was in the process of realizing his art. And perhaps she was too. They were living out their deepest sexual fetishes.

He tensed as she held his erection firmly in the chopsticks, just beneath his circumcised helmet. She began to vibrate the chopsticks so that a series of tremors ran deliciously from the base of his scrotum to the tip of his cock. It was like she was eating him. She began to take the crown of his penis into her heart-shaped mouth. She nibbled at it, running her tongue round and round the eye. But she wouldn't swallow it, wouldn't gag on its enormity.

She teased it with a film of mauve lipstick. She played with it as though she was mixing a colour. She flicked her pigment on to his head and worked it in with the tip of her tongue. And then she resumed with the chopsticks, moving them marginally down his shaft so as to have access to more of his cock. The chopsticks had become the perimeters of her sucking. As she adjusted them so she could take more of him into her tiny mouth. There was such a disproportion between the size of his cock and the aperture of her mouth. It was too massive, too hungry. It was like trying to fit a marble column into a sea anemone. But she was succeeding.

The chopsticks began to move down on the base of his penis. She was now working up and down on it with liberal gulps. Inch by inch his giant member was being fed into her mouth. It was the feat of a contortionist. He was watching himself disappear. It was as though he had been castrated. There was just a mauve lipstick blotch at the area where his penis disappeared into a fold of flesh. She had everything now, and had placed the chopsticks right on line with his balls. He was starting to feel his orgasm mount inside. He repressed it, thinking again of the painting he had already prepared on this theme. He had to avoid thinking of the chopsticks or he would have come immediately. She continued to nibble and engorge. She looked up into his eyes, waiting for instructions as to what to do. He motioned to be let out of her mouth, and grew additionally excited on seeing how the lipstick blushes had stained his phallus. He was burning to ride her, and she slid her hand between her legs in anticipation. She was so wet it was like the Niagara Falls were issuing from her crack.

They fell on each other, her legs folding over his shoulders, and his erection pinning her to the bed. She danced beneath his vigorous thrusts. He was aching to come, and her moans were pitched at such a loud intensity that he imagined passengers in a low-flying aircraft would hear her screams. They built together towards bursting simultaneous orgasm. Her nails shredded his back as she convulsed again and again on his cock. And for him it was as though he would never stop coming, the orgasm mounted to such degrees of pleasure. The sensation burnt them both and left them drained in each other's arms.

They both knew that this was the prelude to a night in which they would not only have it several times, but also live out the more obsessive of their sexual fantasies. The chopsticks would find further use, and he contemplated the idea of using them as orchestral pieces, one inserted into her pussy and one in her bottom. He would jointly sensitize her two passages with these bland eating utensils. He would hear words come from her mouth that he had never heard before, vowels and consonants created by a response to perverse ecstasy. And he would tape it all and replay her vocables in solitude.

But for the moment she pulled on her violet silk panties, and said to him, 'Please take me to the studio. It was where we were headed before finding ourselves here. I still want to see your paintings.'

He led her up the next flight of stairs, and opened the door to his studio, threw a switch and watched as she confronted the large painting which was central to the room as an unfinished work in progress. What she saw was what they had just performed. A woman on her haunches, holding a pair of chopsticks which enveloped a mushrooming penis, was applying a lipsticked mouth to its head. A single hand, which appeared to belong to nobody, the figure and the arm being out of the picture, was seen tickling her from behind.

The girl laughed, while he fitted his hand into the back of her panties. 'I want to do it with you involving every colour lipstick,' he said. 'Orange tomorrow night, brown the next, shocking pink on Sunday. We'll invent our own colour ritual.'

'Only don't come to Harvey Nichols to buy them,' she laughed, 'or I won't be able to work all day. I'll be shivering for more. I'll be so wet I'll have to go to the Ladies Room.'

'Shall we say orange for tomorrow night?' he said. 'And you bring the chopsticks.'

'Fine,' she whispered, as their need started up all over again on the studio floor. They positioned themselves in front of the painting, and he, as he began recircling a lipstick on her clitoris, looked up at the imaginary world he had never thought would become a reality, while she threw her head to one side in abandon, took hold of a chopstick in her mouth, and surrendered herself to play like a kitten.

Devil's Paradise

He had to convince himself that he was really there. As a child he'd dreamt of desert islands, their white crescent beaches washed by turquoise shallows. The one occupant on the beach, a curvaceous Latin girl dressed in nothing but a black sequinned thong, would get up from a scarlet towel and walk to meet him across the sands. She would know everything about him, and their kiss would be spontaneous, tasting of passion fruit, mango and vanilla. He would pick her up and carry her laughing towards the red towel and make love to her under a blindingly blue sky.

He had lived with that vision. And by some freak he had found himself in such a place, only the scantily dressed Latin girl, with her luxurious hair falling in a cobalt waterfall to her waist, was accompanied by an androgyne, a man so feminine that he had to revise his initial impression of seeing two girls, and detail by detail accustom himself to the realization that he was looking at an edifying beach girl accompanied by a man of ambivalent sex.

He had been canoeing offshore, following the current in a whip's sinuous arc round the coast, when he had found himself being pulled out to sea, the victim of a rip-current that left him helpless, oars retrieved from the water, and the sea hurrying beneath the light craft like a downward escalator. He couldn't be sure how long the transitional passage had lasted, it was like he was in trance and out of it, and then suddenly he had heard the sound of waves building to surf and running inshore with white frisky manes. His passage to the shore might have lasted minutes, hours or years. He couldn't tell.

And there they were, the two of them, sharing a violet-coloured towel, and she in heart-shaped dark glasses, her prominent breasts hardly contained by a white bikini top, her full bottom barely covered by a high-cut counterpart on strings, her mouth coloured like a bruised ruby, and her oiled waist tricked across by a thin gold chain, throwing her head over her shoulder to meet his arrival. He could see that the androgynous figure was wearing a pink boa and a pink glitter thong, and was concentrating on what looked to be a spread of fashion glossies.

'I'm Tristran,' he found himself saying, 'I'm from the mainland, and I don't know how I got here. I was taking a course along the coast and suddenly I was being rushed out to sea.'

'You're like all of them,' the androgyne said. 'You'd be surprised how many of you end up here. And sometimes it takes months to get back. This is Loredana.' And Tristran found himself making direct eye contract with the beautiful woman who had pushed her heart-shaped glasses up into her blue-black hair, and sat there looking at him with smouldering intensity. He couldn't help noticing how her left nipple had slipped free of the bikini cup, and the magenta splash it created made him imagine her sex as a similar colour, a tight rosebud concealed by a white bikini gusset. She didn't speak, she just moistened her lower lip with her tongue and looked at him, ran her eyes over his body like two insects, and smiled provocatively. And it was as if her eyelashes had brushed his cock, and were still flickering on his engorged shaft.

'Now that you're here,' the androgyne said, 'you'd better come with us to the villa. It's called "Fly Spotter's Paradise". You'll find out why later.'

Tristran followed the couple across a pristine white beach, his jealousy excited by the fact that the androgyne slipped a finger down the back of Loredana's white bikini bottom, and rested it in her crack. She expressed no emotion at his gesture; Tristran imagined she was darting invitations at his eyes from behind her heart-shaped glasses. She was sultry, decadent, voluptuous in a stylized way, and already he was imagining the sound of her voice as it would throatily plead in its desperate ascent to orgasm. He wanted to spread her legs across the width of the beach and mount her with a cock so marble-hard that it would remain up until she begged to be set free. He had her in mind as a sex slave. A woman who would crawl naked across the floor, her hands tied by a black silk scarf, and pick up strawberries in her lips from a plate left on the floor.

When Loredana spoke it was to point out a particular shade of blue in the sea sky. She said the colour reminded her of childhood, and of sitting on the beach in Sicily listening to pop songs on the radio, and wondering who she would grow up to be. She had a dreaminess about her that made her eroticism more compelling. Tristran kept glancing at the liberties the androgyne was taking with her bottom, for he had extended his hand right down the curve of her bottom to her pussy. It made Loredana roll her hips as she walked.

'What's this island called?' Tristran enquired.

'Devil's Paradise,' said the androgyne, pronouncing it in a way that emphasized the satanic implications. 'People used to come here to perform sex rites, and there's an aphrodisiac mushroom grows in one of the coves that at one time caused men to spend their whole lives navigating the seas to find this paradise. But, as you've discovered, coming here is largely spontaneous; you just arrive, if you ever do, due to some magnetic attraction. The aphrodisiac was known to all sex cults. It is said that it so enhances and prolongs orgasm that a man can come for a full hour in sustained pleasure, for it takes that period of time for the semen to leave the cock. The sensation is so prolonged and overwhelming that men and women lose consciousness under is effects. And for a woman, and Loredana has experienced it, a quantity of the powder brushed into the clitoris and vaginal lips just prior to the man's entry creates correspondingly sustained orgasm. Loredana convulsed in sexual spasm for two hours. It makes you want to fuck like crazy, and each time you get to a pitch of excitement, so it intensifies and you grow more delirious.'

'I imagine it's exceedingly rare,' said Tristran. 'Do you have some at the villa?'

'Wait and see,' said the androgyne, and Loredana laughed in a knowing way.

They crossed the beach and walked in the direction of a grove of trees which obscured the white walls of a beach villa. Tristran could hear the sea behind them, the waves expiring in a slow measured cadence of surf. He could have been anywhere, but he was on Devil's Paradise. He could feel the anticipation mounting in his abdomen. The very air created sexual excitement in him. A heady perfume enveloped the beach, and Tristran thought he could hear a woman's excited laughter issuing through the eucalyptus trees.

The androgyne released his hand from Loredana's round bottom, the bikini bottom having slipped halfway down her tanned cheeks, and Tristran entered a room with a blue marble floor, refreshingly cool to his feet. The room was heaped with silk cushions and couches. There were mauve, green, blue, red and black cushions, and a number of hookahs for smoking opium were placed on small tables. The room led away to others, chiffon curtains dividing the house into sections. And it was now that Tristran could hear the woman's laughter distinctly. She must have been making love in the next room, and her voice was mounting in urgency.

The androgyne came back with a bottle of champagne and three glasses, and Loredana sat curled up on a pile of black cushions, her bikini straps snaking down her bronzed arms. Her mouth was an arrangement of crushed raspberries.

'You asked about the aphrodisiac,' said the androgyne. 'All newcomers to the island are obliged to take it. Excruciating pleasure will be yours a little later. You have to prepare yourself mentally to take the drug. If you recollect your most pleasurable orgasm and multiply that by a million, it will give you some small insight into this compound. It is best taken internally and applied externally to the skin of the penis. And to imagine the sensation externally, you have to think of a hundred thousand ants running up and down your cock as an irritant.'

Tristran watched as Loredana casually took off her bikini top and let her full perfectly conical breasts flop into her lifted hands. She weighed them with sensual fingers, while the androgyne opened a lacquered pill box and decanted a black powder into a tiny saucer. 'Just one grain of the substance,' he noted, 'will intensify orgasm a hundred times,' and as he spoke Tristran could hear the woman's voice next door shrieking with pleasure: no sooner had one shriek risen to its highest sustained pitch, than another would begin, like a series of waves cresting and crashing on the beach. Tristran knew without asking that the woman had taken the aphrodisiac and was experiencing nymphomaniacal orgasm. His own visible excitement at the woman's pleasure mounted in his body, and it was difficult for him to conceal the erection that was poking out above the elasticated band of his lycra swimming trunks. There was Loredana, brushing a few granules of the black powder across her nipples, and pushing her tongue out between red glossed lips.

'Let me tell you why this villa is called "Fly Spotter's Paradise",' said the androgyne. 'It's named after a peculiar fetish of mine.' Tristran watched as the androgyne slipped out of his pink glitter thong, and exposed a throbbing erection. But whereas the man's body flesh was white, so his cock was black.

'What I do,' the androgyne said, 'is to prepare a clear gel from the aphrodisiac, and to have Loredana coat my cock with it like a lacquer. This provides a protection to the skin, but at the same time attracts a particular sort of iridescent fly which settles on the surface. The friction of all these tiny legs and wings eventually makes me come. The build-up is so slow that it may take an hour or even two to come. The longer the better, as the pleasure is more sustained. I've experimented with many different solutions to attract all manner of diverse insects, but it's this one particular fly which allows me to reach ecstatic pleasure.'

Loredana nibbled the androgyne's cock, and then began applying a clear gel from an aquamarine phial to the erection she was so expertly flicking with her tongue. She lacquered the shaft and the androgyne's balls, and already Tristran could hear the audible buzz of flies spotting on the air. They landed on the androgyne's cock like emerald sequins with scintillating legs and wings. They arrived one by one, and gradually there was a blackening squall of them on his erection, the insects crawling over each other in their greed to get at the gel. And the ones who landed directly on the lacquer were detained by the stickiness, and the struggle of their legs and wings to get free enhanced the pleasure that the prostrate androgyne received. He lay back with his cock sticking up like a black totem pole, his eyes closed in ecstasy. And the insects exchanged places. As some flew away gorged on the gel, so others which had been circling in readiness took their place in the vibrant glinting net they formed over the androgyne's erection. And he held his cock at the base like a monolith being offered to pleasure.

Loredana ran one painted fingernail inside the band of her bikini bottom, and told Tristran to prepare for ecstasy. She took up the little saucer of black powder, spooned most of the contents into a glass of ouzo, and placed it in front of Tristran. 'Lick my nipples,' she urged him, and his tongue snake-danced across her violet areolas. Her breath was hot on his shoulder, and her lips began picking at the tender flesh in his ear lobes. He caught fire as he felt her run a single finger along his taut cock.

'Now watch me,' she said, and she took a little of the powder on the point of a finger and brushed it into his cock. And as she did so, it felt like she had ignited all the nerve points in his body. Sensation was so unbearably magnified that he didn't think he would withstand the intensity. 'Now brush a little on my pussy,' she whispered in a purring voice, her fingers slipping down her bikini bottom. She threw her head back against the pile of cushions and opened her legs wide with total abandonment. 'After you've powdered my lips, drink the little glass of solution I've prepared.'

Tristran looked across at the androgyne who moaned with pleasure periodically. His cock was like a green jewel of struggling insects. He had never seen anyone so abandoned, to such perverse pleasure. The insects were choreographing a sexual dance on his penis. And the androgyne made not a movement to accelerate his pleasure. He left everything to the progress of the flies. The head of his cock was a wriggling green helmet. He was in a bitter-sweet agony of allowing his ejaculation to build so slowly that he savoured each second of increasing sensation.

Tristran smeared a finger with black powder and brushed it on Loredana's moist clitoris. She shivered in exacting spasms. Her body was an undulating ripple of curves waiting to arch beneath his entry. He picked up the little glass and swallowed the mixture of ouzo and aphrodisiac. He felt his body respond immediately to the psychoactive compound. His mind was enflamed with erotic imaginings. He saw the sky full of girls sitting in lascivious positions with their legs wide open. He heard penises explode like volcanoes showering the landscape with molten lava. And he knew that when he came it would be eruptive and incandescent, just like an angry volcano.

'There's all the time in the world,' he heard Loredana say as he entered her, and felt her body respond to him like a silk flower. Never before had he known such sensitivity in his genitals. Each thrust of his cock seemed to travel the length of a sinuous river. He knew he was on a journey to sensual paradise. The exchange of the powder on his cock with that at the entrance to her vagina created an impossible frisson of pleasure. Tristran could feel the orgasm mounting in him, but he knew it would take hours to escape. And Loredana was beginning to moan with orgasmic abandon. He pushed her legs right over her shoulders and licked the soles of her feet to increase her ecstasy. She was so overtaken by pleasure that her eyes were closed in a state of semi-trance. And as his own orgasm built it felt like he had been coming since the moment he entered her swollen pussy.

He glanced across at the androgyne whose deep breathing was an indication that his pleasure was rising. He was breathing like a man running up a steep hill. The iridescent flies were working away at the lacquer coating his cock. Loredana too opened her eyes and glanced across at her lover. He was struggling with electric expectation.

Tristran began to thrust deeper. He felt inspired to love every centimetre of her curved body, to navigate the Mississippi inside Loredana's body. He ached with excruciating pleasure, and it was impossible to free himself from the sustained pressure. And he could sense with almost unnatural sensitivity that the degree of her build-up was equal to his own. They were caught in a flailing convoluted knot that wouldn't break.

They heard the androgyne cry out that he was about to come, and Tristran saw the man's body convulse with sweat and ecstasy as a high stream of hot pearls erupted from his cock.

Tristran had no idea how long he and Loredana had been making love. Her tempestuous demands seemed unending, and when he finally came it was like every sexual fantasy and longing in his body exploded at that moment. He collapsed soon afterwards into a sleep in which he imagined that he and Loredana were floating back to the mainland on a big white cloud.

When he awoke, Loredana and the androgyne were sitting on cushions passing a hookah between them. Everything was silent except for a frisky breeze out in the trees, and the sound of waves printing white thunder across the beach.

'No one is permitted to extend their stay at Devil's Paradise,' said the androgyne looking direct into Tristran's eyes. 'Now that you have tasted the aphrodisiac mushroom you must return before you become addicted to its properties. And who knows, one day the sea may bring you here again, and you will resume a life that you will grow in time to think you imagined.'

Loredana moved over and sat in her lover's lap. This woman looked at him now as though they had never made love. He could see that he was to be excluded from their shared life.

'May I take a little of the powder?' he asked, but he knew he would never be allowed to return to the mainland with the aphrodisiac. He wondered about the effects it would have on his girlfriend, and then drank the glass of champagne they offered him before leaving.

It was getting on towards evening. There was an orange and pink glow to the sky. A few stars could be seen sprinkled across the fluid curve of the horizon. His canoe had been placed near the edge of the water. He walked towards it. He had no idea in which direction to row in search of the mainland.

He dragged the canoe into the waves, and looked round a last time. He could hear the agonized screams of a woman building towards orgasm. And with a pang of jealousy as he put out into the surf, he knew the voice was Loredana's.

A Boa Constrictor Tamed by a Flower

There was a bridge that led directly across the ponds, and the few dinghies tied up there had begun to fill with spatulate autumn leaves. It was there that Billy used to encounter this big guy waiting for him, silent, minatory, and imposing: he just stood there evaluating the smaller boy's cock and buttocks through his skintight jeans. It had grown to be a ritual, the big one's musculature hulked on the bridge, his eyes scanning the lacquered shimmer of a leaf-green pond, and the little guy's crossing over to a friend's house on the other side. Billy sensed that there was a weird subtext at work in the body-builder's chemistry, and that the man was moving towards confrontation. It would happen sooner or later, and the sexual energies at work would demand weird erotic rites. Billy also had something on this man.

It happened on a Thursday. The leaves were beginning to rain down on the bridge like shoals of tropical fish, all glossy skins and stalks for tails. Something within Billy wanted to incite provocation, and he took advantage of the mellow October day to dress in black lycra shorts, accompanied by a denim top. He brushed his eyes with dark green mascara, applied a light foundation to his face, and looked out of his bedroom window to find the big guy standing at his usual post on the bridge, one hand rubbing his cock through jeans, the other positioned loosely on a hip. Billy guessed that the man was on steroids and working out, for his voluminous muscles were unnaturally disproportionate to his frame.

Billy started to cross the bridge, using a path rarely taken by pedestrians, and as he did so, he saw the big guy cross his arms and take up a confrontational stance at the other end. He kept on walking, determined not to be intimidated by his evident opponent. Billy felt the adrenalin shooting through his veins; he was fired up for the encounter. He got within ten yards of the man and stood his ground.

'Hi there, cutie,' the big guy drawled. 'Where do you think you're going looking like a faggot? I want a word with you.'

Billy stopped short. The man was wearing a white T-shirt and blue jeans with a button-fly like a sailor's. He was all remonstrance and hard posturing. And there were two red circular blotches on his T-shirt at the level of the nipples. Billy wondered about these coronas, and heard the man say, 'I've been watching you for a long time. We need to get to know each other. I'm the man here, and you're the woman.'

'I don't think so,' Billy replied. 'You're the woman and I'm the man, and I'll prove it.'

The big guy smiled. He kept his hand over his genitals, but Billy couldn't make out the outline of a taut erection. It was like the man was posturing with little to offer. There was a blue gel in his short black hair, and it was clear that he devoted fastidious care to his appearance.

'I'm in a hurry,' Billy said, 'I've got to be at a friend's house in a few minutes.' Billy knew that he said the words with little conviction, and that their meeting would naturally evolve into a sexual rite.

'I didn't think body-builders wore lipstick,' he said to the man. 'You've got it round your nipples, haven't you!'

The man smiled. 'Call me Rachel,' he said. His undertones were still menacing, though given a self-deprecatory edge by the marginal dissatisfaction he felt with his gender role. Billy felt that Rachel wanted to dominate him, but lacked the potency suggested by his musculature to be the active male. There was something depotentized about Rachel, and Billy with his heightened sensitivity guessed it would be steroids, and that the latter would result in his having a limp dick. All that expansively developed frame would terminate in a defused potential.

'Haven't we met before?' Billy said, feeling his cock trigger. 'You must remember that hotel room in Tangier. You were tied up in chains on the bed, while two or three youths had their way with you. I was the guy with the camera.'

Billy watched the consternation spread across Rachel's face, and knew that he had gone far enough. He had the man alerted to a web of complicitous guilt, and all the more powerful in that his only release would be through the violence he wouldn't dare project.

'You've got the wrong guy,' Rachel said. 'But I'll show you a thing or two in that boating-shed over there. I can lift you on my cock all day.'

Billy felt the pulse drumming in his abdomen, a sort of manic sun shooting impulses through his veins. He was correspondingly compelled and repelled by the man's perfectly developed torso. The man had the sinuousness of a big cat, a panther or jaguar. There were jungle storms and lightnings concealed in his chest, stampeding beasts lived in his pectorals. Billy found himself following the man, and walking in a state of sexual trance towards the open boating-shed, its wooden doors peeling, and red and yellow leaves splashing the entrance. The whole path by the pond looked like a membrane of stained glass.

It was dark inside the shed, and Rachel closed the door behind them. Light leaked in through a window in the roof, but Rachel knew the place and switched on a lamp that stood on a wooden bench. The air smelled of petrol, tar, boating things, and musty decaying scents. Billy warmed to the dark, oily intimacy that the place afforded. The size of his own cock was legendary, and for someone of such slight stature, it grew from him like a proboscis. He felt it hammering against the black lycra skin which contained it.

'Want to wrestle?' Rachel drawled, shaping up a muscle in his right arm to a convex globe.

Billy lightly dabbed at the bigger man's torso; he felt like a midget in the presence of some mythic giant's undulating bulk. 'Don't forget I've got the photos,' he admonished. 'You're caught in some compromising scenes, Rachel. Do you remember those street boys. Three of them fucked you, and you wore a leather face-mask so you wouldn't be recognized. But I recognize you, Stephen. It's Stephen, isn't it, when you're not Rachel?'

The big guy's defences were coming down. Billy could see that the man was a passive slave waiting to be broken into by his cock. He would have him crawl naked on all fours across the bench, simulating an odalisque, her bottom polished with oil, and a tantalizing ruby on a chain suspended at her waist.

Rachel lifted up his white T-shirt to reveal two erect nipples polished by scarlet lipstick. Billy could see that the guy was really excited by the idea of being seen like this, and that his kicks came from empathizing with his partner's excitement. And Billy guessed that there was lipstick highlighting other parts of Rachel's body, and button by button he began undoing Rachel's denim fly, poking a finger periodically and coaxingly through the interstices, and still discovering no erection, no well-hung baton pumping to an engorged girth. What he had in his hands was someone submissive as a houri, a steroid artefact waiting to be fucked.

Billy got Rachel's jeans down to his ankles, and he stepped out of them. His own cock was beating a percussive rhythm at his waist. Rachel was in the tiniest black briefs, and his voluminous genitals hung pendant in that pouch.

Rachel went down on Billy's erection, wrapping his tongue round the head, and playing its fingerstops like an oboe. Billy worked his hands into Rachel's wall of shoulder muscles, and knew that he could humiliate the man as a slave. He would answer every peremptory dictate, no matter how avengingly bizarre.

'Get down on all fours,' Billy commanded, and he slid Rachel's black briefs down to discover a lipstick circle drawn around and across the crack of his buttocks. The line was in the same poppy-red colour as that drawn to accentuate his nipples.

'I'll fuck you so hard it will be like a stampede of elephants,' Rachel disclosed, attempting to apologize for his vulnerable passivity.

'You're on so many steroids, you couldn't get it up an inch,' Billy let out, as he manoeuvred his penis into the lipstick circle, taunting Rachel with his slow exploratory expertise, working it on the bud and then backing off, and then repeating his provocative enquiry.

Rachel was beginning to plead for penetration, a boa constrictor tamed by a flower. 'Before you get this,' Billy said, 'you're going to swear to me you'll act honest, and stop intimidating people like me. I know you, Stephen. I keep tracks on guys like you,' and simultaneously thrusting deep into Rachel's anus and impaling him with his cock, Billy reached for the shoulder bag he had kept within arm's reach, and grabbed at his camera.

Now he had him. Balancing on Rachel, he began snapping pictures of their union, and of the man's feminized bottom, riding him like a bronco-buster standing up in the saddle. He'd take the risk of fighting for his camera afterwards, but for the moment submitted to the sexual combat. The rapacious snake and undulating flower ran through his head as a recurring image. It was just that, and all he could hear was Rachel instructing him, 'Deeper, go deeper,' and a wind kicking up the leaves outside.

Alice through the Looking Glass

Alice lived in the restored wing of an otherwise vacated gothic mansion on the edge of the city. She arched her legs in the voluminous marble bath, pushed them up vertical, as though they were being appraised by the posters of Elvis Presley and the Marquis de Sade on the opposite wall, and then with her head supported on the rim, kicked them back over her shoulders. She liked to tickle herself in this posture, her pussy dripping with scented foam, and to imagine a spectator observing her through the two-way mirror her uncle had ingeniously incorporated into the bathroom restoration. Alice fantasized that she was being watched. The spectator would be cupping his balls with his left hand, and working on his cock with the right. He would modulate his virtuoso rhythm, anxious to restrain his crisis until the exact moment when Alice cried out from her solitary pleasure. And her red fingernails worked slowly, expertly over her shaved pussy, the little jewel that she depilated with such extreme attention to detail. She dipped her forefinger in and wriggled. If only Presley, in his skintight hipsters, would step down off the wall, unzip and mount her without a word of introduction, or Sade come out of his formal eighteenth-century pose, and brandish a cane across her soft, nubile buttocks.

Alice had just turned eighteen but she looked considerably younger, and liked to put her hair in ribboned plaits, and to wear a pleated micro-skirt which emphasized her long, curvy legs. Her uncle called her his divine cock-teaser, and Alice never objected to his following her up the tall staircase, staying back a number of stairs the better to see all the way up her disarmingly short skirt. She got moist from that little game; and several times on his return from lengthy stays abroad, she had opportunely walked out of the bedroom in her black bra and panties to find him stationed in the corridor, as though already anticipating her flouncily provocative streak to the bathroom.

Was someone outside now, she asked herself, as she began to quicken the rhythm of her fingers, her voice starting to rise as she felt her pleasure increasing. It was excruciating. She ached with the fantasy of having a thick cock pushed into her now, right on the edge of orgasm. Or better, two. She would gag on the smooth columnar one, while a knottier heavy weapon pinned her with its remorselessly vigorous thrusts.

Alice heard her throaty scream of pleasure. She had forgotten, or half forgotten, that her uncle's parasitical valet, Frank, was still in, and probably lying on his bed flicking through the girlie magazines he collected from the fifties and sixties. She had discovered boxes of vintage *Playboy* and pin-up magazines in Frank's wardrobe. The shots were more discreetly posed than today's nudes, and Frank was clearly obsessed by the variety of stocking shots available to the reader, most of the models emphasizing the seductive appeal of seamed stockings and suspenders.

Alice wondered about Frank. She knew of his preference for wearing false eyelashes, and she had been tempted to leave a pair of her used black knickers on his pillow to see what response this action would provoke. Frank must have been a youthful forty, and it had been his job to drive her to and from school in her uncle's Bentley. It was then she had acquired the provocative backseat poses of a teenage tart. Defying school regulations by wearing white see-through panties under her gymslip, Alice had sat reading in the rear of the car, her legs arched in a way that allowed Frank to see everything in the driving mirror. On the road home she would apply eye make-up, and with her legs angled over the empty front passenger seat, and her hem retreating to the area of her hips, she would read Sade's *Justine* as the car hummed through the lanes leading to their gothic retreat.

Alice sank back into the bath in the afterglow of her sustained pleasure. It had never occurred to her that Frank might be intimate with her uncle's system of two-way mirrors, and that he could at this moment be observing her masturbatory ritual in the bath. Far from repulsing her, the thought made her tingle with pleasure. She would make her emergence from the bath, and the subsequent process of getting dressed, a protracted and tantalizing one.

Alice stepped out of the bath nurturing the pretence that Frank was watching her, and began teasingly to dry herself with a towel, presenting her round pink bottom to the voyeur's eye as she bent down in pursuit of an imaginary hairpin. He would see right up her crack. She was saving her little trick of pencilling a beauty spot on her right buttock until later. If Frank was out there wanking, he would shoot up his nostrils at the sight of that precocious ornamentation of her bum. Alice busied herself in the mirror, plucking an eyebrow into a pencilled arch, and spending a lot of time studying her sensitively refined features. She placed two violet ribbons in her plaits to accentuate her schoolgirlishness, and then applied a sensuous oil to her thighs, her shaved pubic triangle, and more leisurely and demonstratively, into her glowing buttocks. If Frank was watching, his cock would be in his fist, stiff as a policeman's baton. Alice then proceeded to dress with a pashir's enticement. She snapped on a black translucent bra, and then worked her black see-through panties up from the ankles to the backs of her legs, all the way up until the transparent fabric was filmed tightly against her bottom. She patted her cheeks saucily, and ran a fingernail down the length of her crack. She then fastened her black suspender belt around her waist, dabbed perfume behind her knees, put on her lipstick as a vivaciously flirtatious insignia, buttoned up a red silk blouse, put on a tiny pleated mini, and decided to leave the rolling on of her stockings until later. Already, she felt like fingering herself again. The process of dressing up always had her moist. Alice was perpetually slippery at the crotch. Deciding to pursue her fantastic game to the end, she sat back in the bathroom chair and elongated then bent her leg to the knee as she slipped on a seamed stocking, manoeuvring it from the knee up until the black stocking top was secured by the suspender fastening. She sat with one leg down and one arched, and then repeated the process on the left leg, standing up to check the vertical alignment of her seams. If Frank was watching he would have fisted his semen into an ejaculatory plume by now, a hot ribbon of percolated lust. Alice delayed a moment, then slipped out into the corridor, and as she did she was certain she heard a bedroom door close. Frank must have slipped back to his lair, either enflamed or appeased by what he had seen.

Alice was in the mood to tart it up, she was simmeringly restless, and slipping on her spike heels she rapped past Frank's door with an exaggerated staccato click. She felt the impulse to run her heels abradingly down his spine and knead them into his taut buttocks. Instead, she went to her room, and slammed the door. Another Presley poster was looking down at her from above the bed, and she flicked a finger over his crotch, and insolently stuck out her tongue at the immortalized star.

She collapsed on her bed and thought of Steve, the schoolboy whose virginity she had taken by blowing him on his mother's bed. She had tormented him by refusing him access to her pussy, and then shocked him by an oral expertise that had him convulsing in paroxysmal ecstasy on his mother's silk counterpane. And after deep-throating him to near orgasm, she had disengaged his penis at the moment of climax and his come had shot all over the counterpane. And leaving him no time in which to recover from the confusion of the situation, she had abruptly exited from the room, and had never dated him again. Alice was living out her uncle's epithet of being a divine cock-teaser.

Bored by her life of idleness and luxury, Alice was in search of sensation. Her uncle wasn't due back from South America for another week, so she lacked a dinner companion, and someone whose conversation about the bizarre, the weird and the wonderful, helped assuage the feverish excitement with which she anticipated a hedonistic future. Several times she had sat at the table fingering herself while her uncle alluded to encounters in the red-light districts of innumerable capitals. On another occasion she had come to the table wearing crotchless knickers under her skirt, so that her furtive access to vicarious pleasure should go unimpeded. Pussy juice had trickled sweetly down her thighs with the scent of guava.

Alice itched in her see-through panties. She spread her legs and fantasized. She wondered how Frank would take her, would he put her up on her haunches, or would he command her on top with his omnipotent possession of her body? Anyhow, she would enact her plan. She listened attentively to hear when Frank would leave his room, and at an opportune moment when he slipped out to the bathroom, Alice sped into his room with a pair of unwashed black silk knickers she had fished out of her washing bag, and placed the choice item on Frank's pillow, in such a way that he would instantly recognize the wearer. The rankly perfumed fetish was a knicker-collector's paradise, and Alice imagined Frank fitting the intimately scented silk to his vibrant erection. She sucked her thumb in anticipation, and curled up on the bed in a Lolita pose, tracing a finger over her lower left buttock, and extending it to that whole erogenous zone. Alice wished she could elongate her neck sufficiently to lick her own pussy, and to lap at her fidgety clit.

She heard Frank return to his room, and the door clicked shut. Silence washed over the house again like a lake rising on itself. Alice scratched at her knickers a couple of times and waited. There was no way in which Frank could ignore a black triangle draped over his pillow. Panties were recognizable anywhere, even if you encountered them in the most unlikely places, like dropped out of somebody's laundrette bag on to the pavement, or accidentally pulled out of a jacket pocket when searching for a pen. Alice waited. She was so wet she sat in a slick of juices, but she refrained from rubbing herself in the hope that Frank would come to her room.

She put on her headphones and listened to an old Donna Summer CD, before growing suddenly aware of a knock at the door. Alice had deliberately laddered her stockings in order to heighten her tartishness, and she strutted over to the door and opened it so that she was concealed to the caller. She waited, and Frank walked tentatively into the room. He was dressed in nothing but her tiny black knickers, his cock straining over the elasticated band, and he had brushed his false eyelashes with mascara. He looked like a transvestite slut, and it was clear to Alice that he had come to teach her a lesson. Frank had never to her eyes looked so sexually assertive.

Alice shut the door and followed him into her room. She wolf-whistled at the wiggle of Frank's ass, her black bikini knickers cutting into his white flesh. The conspiratorial atmospherics in the room were like the preconceived culmination to a rite that both had been planning for years. 'You want to be fucked, you little hooligan,' Frank said, and it was the first time Alice had ever heard him speak out of character. 'Your knickers will soon be soggy when I stretch your cunt. Don't think I haven't seen you dressing and undressing in the bathroom, scratching your twat, and pencilling beauty spots on your bum. Alice through the looking glass should be your cock-teasing name.'

Alice loved hearing Frank talk dirty, and she rolled compliantly on the bed, and began to tease him by running a red fingernail over the crotch of her see-through panties.

Frank flipped her over, and roundly spanked her wriggling schoolgirl's bottom. 'Not so simple,' he said. 'Go into the bathroom, and sit in the chair and finger yourself, and I'll watch in the mirror.' Alice duly complied, spreading her legs and working herself to feverish orgasm, her voice crying out with frustration and pleasure.

'Come out, you little tart,' Frank dictated, and Alice pushed her skirt down, clicked to attention with her heels, and scurried back into the corridor. She looked all in a flutter, and with her hair in mauve ribbons, she resembled an excited schoolgirl. 'Into my room,' Frank demanded, and Alice entered Frank's domain which, except for a few bottles of spirits and a generous sprinkling of her stolen knickers like trophies across the bed, was a strictly masculine space. There was a scent of cologne in the room and *Playboy* magazines were stacked in archival boxes. Alice sensed a conspiratorial link between Frank and her uncle; in fact, she half expected her uncle to appear at any moment in one of his elegant silk kimonos, his cock projecting horizontally from a fold in the silk. The result would have been a long, complicated fuck, extending three ways until dawn.

'Lick me, you teenage cocksucker,' Frank commanded. 'Get down on your knees and shampoo my dick, bitch.' Alice was greedy to obey, and she slid to her knees and began licking the cock she had disengaged from her own black knickers. She tongued him from the base of his scrotum to the tip of his cock. She wolfed him down with hot rapacity, a salacious smile consuming her features. She worked on him with a consummate knowledge gained from sampling schoolboys' cocks on so many backseats of cars, and from assimilating any number of erotic videos. There was no end to the culinary art of head.

Frank backed off from her gorging lips. He wanted to prolong the pleasure of seeing Alice on heat. He would like to have sat under a glass table and observed the whole geometry of her pudenda from that level, the depilated lips spread open for his enquiry, the shaved crack terminating in her tight anal bud.

Alice awaited her next command. She went down on her knees with her bottom thrust out, and stared up at Frank, all the time rolling her tongue over her lips as though she was still engorging his cock. It was a weird reversal of roles, with Alice acting as sexual factotum to a man who was generally paid to look after her welfare. 'Why don't you fuck me, you wanker,' she hissed at him, and his face crumpled into a condescending smile. His cock was prodding vertically at his belly button, but this man had all the time in the world, and wasn't going to settle for something as simple as a straight fuck. Alice knew she was totally at his disposal, and no immediate moves on his cock would make any impression unless he instigated the action. She was confronting a stranger, and not her uncle's valet, and a stranger possessed of a complex sexual repertoire. Frank, who spent his life obeying orders, was suddenly in direct command of this sexual game.

He commanded Alice to sit on the bed. 'You'll get fucked later,' he said, 'but first I want my pleasure. Take off a stocking and fit it like a condom over my cock.' Alice fitted Frank's cock to the toepiece of her nylon. 'Now place my cock inside your shoe,' and Alice fitted the nyloned head into her pointed stiletto. 'That's it,' moaned Frank. 'Now work me off and finger yourself,' Frank demanded, and Alice rubbed Frank's cock in and out of her pointed leather shoe as though the latter was her pussy. When he came it was volcanic, and after a pause he was ready to give her what she wanted. Alice kicked her legs up. Her toes were in contact with Elvis Presley. It gave her pleasure to think she was masturbating the King, while Frank filled her with the solid cock for which she was aching.

Surf and Sensuality

That summer the water was sapphire and aquamarine in the shallows. The sea bed could be seen as a mosaic of coral, shells, maroon weed, and bright fish flickered in impulsive stops and starts between boulders made visible by the translucent water. When Juliana dived down into that silent marine world, she thought it was like entering a Max Ernst painting, an interior lit up by colours and shapes which seemed to have stepped straight out of the imagination.

It was late afternoon as she sat on the beach, the intense heat of the day over, and luxuriated in a mellow warmth that seemed to make even breathing effortless. She had arranged a red towel and a black one to overlap as though she was sitting in the corolla of a flower. Juliana always stylized her gestures. Her handbag was full of ingredients for little rituals of make-up, and for tiny flourishes that enhanced her femininity.

Two days ago she had met Justin, an underground film maker who had come to Limni in search of inspiration for a film he wanted to shoot called 'Love Amongst the Ruins'. Juliana had felt magnetized to this slim, refined, hyperintense man who entertained her with his bizarre ideas for future films. They had sat talking all afternoon until the sky had turned a deep blue, and then they had gone back to his villa and continued talking until the sky was full of stars. Juliana had felt erotically enflamed by Justin's speech, and she could feel the eroticism in him wound to a tight coil. They had drunk wine together, and once when a red trickle of escaped wine had tracked down Justin's chin, Juliana had withheld the impulse to lick the offending droplets from his stubble. She had fantasized about running her scarlet fingernails over his chest and stomach, and stopping at his waist so as to leave his desire raging.

But when the following day he had come to find her on the beach, again in the late afternoon, he appeared less intimate and was withdrawn into a subjective world to which she had no access. He had appeared moody and singularly lacking in the vivacious charm to which she had been so magnetized on the previous day. None the less, she felt compulsively attracted to this man who carried an aura of mystique with him like a blue halo surrounding his body. She had imagined fastening her lips to him and deepening a kiss that would taste of summer and tingling fruit cocktails. He had told her that he was busy with his thoughts and needed to walk for a long time in order to crystallize the images he had in mind. And despite the fact that she had been topless, her pronounced breasts splashed with mauve anemones for nipples, he had done no more than direct his eyes there, and dressed as always in a white suit and white shirt, he had quickly got up from the sand and walked away along the coast. And although her eyes followed him right to the olive trees through which he disappeared, he never once looked round.

To console herself, Juliana had got up and rushed into the blue sea and stayed there a long time while the water relaxed her, and her mind slowed down from its sensual turmoil. She knew the attraction men felt to her voluptuous curves, and she wondered if Justin was playing games with her, and adopting a moody perverse don't-touch-me attitude in order to increase her sense of passionate longing. When she had reappeared from the surf, she had exchanged her wet bikini bottom for a pair of tiny black silk panties, and smudging a volcanic red glow to her lips she had lain there, face down on her towel, convinced that he was the only man in the world who would reject her in his state of petulant abandon. She ran her hands over her bottom and approved of her curves. Her blond hair fell like sunlight across her shoulders. The beach had been totally deserted.

But now she was waiting with anticipation. She had made herself up with great attention to detail, and the dusty white eye shadow she was wearing perfectly complemented a sultry orange lipstick worn with a black bikini thong. She had painted her toenails orange, and sat on her arrangement of red and black towels. There was no one swimming. She worked UV protective creams into her skin, and stared out at the horizon. The blue of the sea and the sky were indivisible. At a certain point they became the seamless future.

Juliana was impatient. Her holiday was rapidly running out, and there were only another three days available to her before she returned to her job in Fiesole. She felt the need to deepen her knowledge of Justin and the enigmatic life to which he alluded only by evasive hints. Who is this man? she found herself enquiring. And if his past is impenetrable, then perhaps I can add clarity to his future.

She was about to give up on him when she saw his familiar white-suited figure coming across the beach to meet her. Juliana felt so excited that she involuntarily ran a finger slowly across her crotch. She had felt excited ever since yesterday when she had lain face down on the beach in her black panties instead of a bikini bottom. She was again topless, and made no effort to conceal her full breasts from eyes which she knew scrutinized every detail of the world around them.

When he reached her, she could see the excitement in his eyes. 'I've found the place,' he told her. 'The exact location for shooting "Love Amongst the Ruins". And I've decided that you're just the person I need to participate in the film. If we walk out there now, Lucinda will be waiting for us.'

Juliana felt instinctively suspicious of the idea of Lucinda, but refrained from voicing her curiosity. And she was conscious as she bent over to collect her things that Justin's eyes were devouring her full and tanned bottom divided by the thin string of a black thong. She knew she was engaged in the most provocatively exciting of gestures, and took her time searching for a red comb which had become obscured in a towel. It was an additional chance for her to be uncompromisingly stylized, and she knew her bottom was sexily dusted with sand, its granules clinging to traces of oil.

Juliana put on a skimpy red T-shirt and shorts and walked with Justin round the beach, ducked into scrubby foliage and took a path up above the sea. The earth was parched, and the olive trees were a crisp silver. And once when she took the lead in front she felt Justin brush a finger across the top of her thigh. It could have been imagination, but she was convinced it was reality.

They climbed up to the ruins of a marble villa, and a white statue was positioned on a ledge overlooking the sea. Justin must have decorated its head with laurel leaves and red hibiscus flowers, and the armless torso was enhanced by the romantic gesture which embellished its coldly classical features.

'Lucinda,' Justin called, and Juliana was shocked when a woman she might have taken for herself in any crowd walked towards her. It was like confronting herself in a mirror, and she caught her breath. And to confuse the issue, Lucinda was dressed just like her, and was wearing the same red T-shirt and tanga thong that Juliana had adopted as her summer dress. At first Juliana thought she was hallucinating the phenomenon, but Lucinda rucked up her blond hair with a lazy hand, while Juliana assured herself that her left hand was at her side. They were identical look-alikes, even to each having a black band in her hair. And they shared the same figure. Juliana was sure that if Lucinda took off her top, she too would have a beauty spot just above the left nipple, and one on the upper part of the right breast.

Justin offered no explanation, and Juliana put her hands to her head to prevent losing balance. Someone was playing games with her, or was it the heat? She didn't know, but she felt an overwhelming sense of sexual desire for her double. And Justin was right there at her shoulder, his breath caressing her skin.

'But who is this?' she found herself asking, and Justin and her female counterpart both exclaimed, 'Lucinda.' There were two green lizards sunning on a crumbling wall, and one darted into cover like a forked lightning.

Juliana watched as Lucinda slipped from her red T-shirt, and just as she had imagined, her breasts were full like her own, and characterized by the two beauty spots she had thought individual to her. And as though compelled to follow, Juliana too took off her T-shirt and then her skintight shorts and stood facing her rival or friend in the same high-cut thong. And losing consciousness of time and place she had failed to note that Justin was filming events with a camcorder. He had spoken of doing rough preliminaries, and was busy recording the initial relations between the two women.

It was cooler here because of the preponderance of trees, and Juliana sensed that Lucinda was going to kiss her at some stage. They looked directly into each other's eyes.

'I used to be Justin's girlfriend,' Lucinda said. 'He brought you here to convince himself that it wasn't me who was pretending to be you. I know he met you on the beach two days ago. Only by bringing us together would he be convinced that he wasn't resuming his relationship with me. I know the whole thing sounds unreal, but I can assure you it's true. I came to Limni with him as a companion, and somehow he met you. When he came back from the beach yesterday he asked me why I had spent the afternoon on the beach when I assured him I was looking for this ruin. That's how alike we look. Having said this, Lucinda came closer. Juliana felt the warmth of her double's carnation-scented breath as their mouths came together and locked in the sensuous oval of a red kiss. It was like fire flickered into that space, and all the time Juliana was saying to herself, this is the first time I've ever kissed a woman, and it has all the surprise and excitement that I imagined. She could feel a finger which she knew was Justin's tracking down the length of her spine to the crack of her bottom. And then the finger was gone, for he was clearly busy filming this passionate embrace between his ex-lover and the woman he intended to be his new lover.

The two of them stood back, and watched butterflies flickering between the grasses, one white star folding over another in flight. There was an absolute sense of timelessness attached to this place. It was like stepping into a dream of the past.

'I know although you've hardly met, you feel a lot for Justin,' Lucinda said. 'And perhaps you'll continue the relationship I decided to leave. I left Justin because I needed space and time. He was still attracted to me, and so he discovered the closest thing to it, you. But you don't know him well enough yet to undergo the one test which I hope will convince him of our physical difference. I've assured him I will discover the hidden knowledge for him. I have a tiny red love-heart tattoo right next to the fold of my vagina. It's so distinctive to a lover that it could hardly be repeated in anyone else. If you'll let me kiss you there, I can then inform Justin that he has discovered a new girlfriend.'

Juliana found herself complying, and Lucinda led her to a place in a grove of olive trees where contrary to her expectations, Juliana derived pleasure and excitement from the distinguishing examination. Lucinda showed considerable oral expertise, and it was only after aeons had elapsed that the two women emerged from the shade and found Justin sitting with one arm round the partly truncated statue.

'There's no need to even ask me,' Lucinda told him, and she made a hurried departure for an evening date on the island. 'I'm free, and you two are only just beginning.'

Juliana watched her walk away. Justin took her hand and suggested they walk back across the beach to the villa he was renting on the coast. It was cooler now. The beach was still deserted. Juliana was ready for anything. She slipped her arm round his waist, and the seagulls accompanied them, their raucous screams ringing in the empty blue air.

Blue by You

Sunday was the blue day in the week. To Greil it was like an unfinished poem, or a jazz riff remembered from a club somewhere in Berlin, Paris, or London; a sort of inconclusive piece that suggested endless journeys, and pastel-coloured houses facing a bridge over the black undertow of a river's current.

But out walking that afternoon, he remembered the short-skirted librarian, her invitingly long legs terminating in black pointed ankle-boots, her hair tied in a red ribbon the colour of her lipstick, and her big black eyes sheltered behind St Laurent frames. She was the bright constellation in his memory. When he felt about to be extinguished by solitude and the vacuous anonymity of the crowds, he remembered her, as he did at night when his sexual fantasies rioted around her availability as provocative image. He didn't as yet even know her name.

Greil walked quickly along the harbour front. A blond girl in seam-splitting jeans engaged his eyes, and he felt the nerves in his abdomen resonate like a tuned instrument. She walked from her hips, and he watched the quiver of her bottom pronounce a vocabulary of rhythmic provocation. There were some Swedish and Japanese cargo boats berthed in the still docks, and the water was flat and opaquely green. Gulls burst across the sky like an origami trail.

Greil headed up a side street, and listened to his footsteps echo as though they were reverberating on a drum-skin. He intended to head towards a number of cafés in his harbour-front district where young people met on Sunday afternoons, and by the evening spilled on to the pavement, all of them gravitating to the sexual hedonism created by loud music. Greil was hoping to start a liaison, or just pick up someone for the night and see where the encounter took him.

He walked along in a state of high anticipation, a euphoria he always experienced at the onset of possible meetings. Suddenly a door opened and slammed, and two girls hurried down the steps and began walking down the street. Greil couldn't believe it. The girl to the left was the librarian on whom his thoughts had been trained, and she was dressed in a violet-coloured micro-mini which gave full emphasis to her legs, and the black pencil-line seams travelling the length of her sheer tights. She wore black spike heels, and her redheaded friend was moulded into the black banana-skin of lycra leggings. Greil increased his pace slightly, for the girls had set out at a fast walk, and seemed to be headed for the cafés which were his intended destination.

The one he so liked had her hair in a violet band to match her skirt. He caught hints of her perfume, and with his knowledge of the subject he recognized it as Amirage by Givenchy. He was excited by the whole engaging aura that this girl transmitted. He longed to know her name, and to explore her legs; he imagined running the tip of his tongue right up the line of each seam to the mauve bud between her thighs. It would be like travelling parallel highways to a tantalizingly approved point. He imagined she would be wearing tiny mauve panties under her skirt, and he delighted in the thought of having them bunched around one ankle while he coaxed himself into her, pulsating inch by inch.

Greil followed the girls, not intentionally, but by way of their taking the same streets towards the precinct in which the Red Sundown and Blue Port cafés were situated. The girls occasionally reciprocated a vivacious laughter, or linked arms, and were quite unaware of Greil's pursuit at a discreet distance. He was growing acutely fond of this girl to whom he had never properly spoken, and he was inwardly jealous that she could be on the way to a rendezvous with a lover. He kept on telling himself that perhaps the two girls were going to fulfil a date, and that he would end up eating his heart out in one of the dockside bars, seeing everything through a whisky haze, and seeing nothing at all.

There were clouds chasing across the sky: they looked like a herd of bison starting to stampede. Greil could sniff rain in the air, and that would be for later. The girls stopped off at a newsagent, and reappeared with a copy of *Glamour*, and both stood a moment looking at the shot of the French model on the cover before continuing at a staccato, heel-clicking pace towards the Red Sundown.

Greil watched the two go inside. The one he fancied was smoothing down her skirt at the back, checking for the reassurance that she was fully covered. Greil never tired of those little gestures which defined a woman. He kept a detailed inventory of them in his mind, and the pretty librarian manifested every feminine trait that he relished. She could at this moment have no idea of the ways in which she was seducing him, or that he was imagining a minimal triangle of black silk clinging to her curved bottom. He was longing to eroticize the most sensitive centimetres of her clitoris, and to initiate her into pleasures that would have her pleading in submissive postures. In his mind she was already crawling across a piano-top, picking sugar grains off it with her tongue, and later on pecking sugar grains off his cock.

Greil followed the girls into the café. The place was in semi-darkness, and the tables were lit by red lamps. Elvis Presley was singing 'Heartbreak Hotel', and the room was half full. Groups of girls sat at the table, and young men stood up at the bar or against the walls, singling out the ones who attracted their attention. The two girls took up a table near the rear, and Greil found a table conveniently near to theirs. He was all eyes as the librarian sat down, composing her long legs and crossing them in a way that guarded her secret triangle. Greil was fixated by her curvaceousness, and kept expecting that the girls had a pre-arranged date, and that two young men would arrive to interpose themselves between him and his telescopic view up the girl's skirt. The music ached in his veins; he kept on trying to catch the girl's eye, but she was absorbed in the edition of *Glamour*, and she and her friend had formed a microcosm from which he was excluded. He could feel the electric parameters of their closed circle; it jumped out at him like a set of nerves.

Greil thought he was imagining things. It happened simultaneously with his catching sight of a flicker of the girl's black panties, that their eyes met. He assumed he had been caught out in his exaggeratedly close scrutiny of her legs, but the girl's smile acknowledged nothing of his clandestine voyeurism, but instead played directly into his own. It was like catching a chocolate in his mouth. The next moment the girl in the moulded lycra went off to the Ladies Room, and Greil, acting out of his normally shy character, found himself going over to the girl's table, and asking if she would mind if he joined them. Her lips seemed redly inviting. He sat with his legs parallel to hers, and couldn't help wonder what it would be like to have her legs somersaulted over her head, or up on all fours, bottom arched for his tongue to explore her in the 69 position. It would be like licking Turkish Delight.

'I've seen you at the library,' the girl simmered. 'I'm Joanna, and my friend's called Heather.'

'I've been admiring you for a long time,' Greil said. 'It's pure coincidence that we should both end up at the Red Sundown. I suppose you know my interests: modern fiction. Bowles, Burroughs, Genet: that sort of stuff.'

The girl laughed. Greil could almost see the little black triangle of her panties through the fine mesh of her tights. The tension tightened in his abdomen. Their initial rapport was such that he knew he was going to succeed. He imagined her long red fingernails making tracks across his balls. And when Heather returned to the table, there was no strain to the relationship he was beginning to establish with Joanna. With his adrenalin racing, he found himself placing a tentative hand on her right knee, fingers that went unreproved, and stayed there like a cat beginning to play with a mouse.

The café was starting to fill up. A young man came over and started to talk engagingly to Heather, and it was with an elated sense of relief that Greil watched the young man draw up a chair, and make her his centre of attention. It allowed him in turn to concentrate exclusively on Joanna, and he was captivated by the red imprint of her lips on the coffee cup, and the way the lower lip formed the outline of a pinkish crescent moon. Joanna was right up close to him and was telling him a compressed biography of the important events in her past, with the manic rush of someone wanting to impart the lot in a given space of time. She was playfully flirtatious, and took out a compact and checked her lips, and then recrossed her legs, and in repositioning his hand Greil took the advantage of travelling higher up her right thigh. And suddenly, and without any warning, they kissed, their lips rotating in a hot circle before Greil advanced his tongue in a mimetic snake-dance deep into Joanna's palate. Correspondingly he ran his hands over her shoulders and down her spine, and traced out the horizontal ridge of her bra, and then the two shoulder straps, as though he was playfully undressing her. She smudged her lips into his as he began kneading her nipples with the base of his thumbs. He could tell from Joanna's sensually rhythmic response that in private they would take things to an incandescent climax.

'We need a little more privacy,' Joanna breathed into Greil's ear, before she injected her tongue into that helical cavity. 'My flat's quite close to here. Shall we go back there for a drink?'

Together they walked back, and Greil moved his arm from Joanna's waist to her bottom, his hand resting on the violet fabric of her moulded skirt. He was more excited than he could ever remember having been, for he had obsessively entertained the fantasy of converting a librarian into a sex slave. For months he had imagined her climbing up high steps in a micro-skirt, while he stood below tickling her bottom with a long plumed feather, and then with her consulting a book, her glasses tilted forward on the bridge of her nose, and with her concentration absolute, he would begin the process of taking her black panties down inch by inch until they formed a dark pool at her ankles. And then detaching them from her spike heels, and with her still absorbed in a point of reference, he would climb up the steps and tie her hands. That done, he would begin licking her upwards from the backs of her feet to her pussy, leg by leg as though he was following the lines of stocking seams. He had fantasized about doing this to Joanna, and had imagined the undulating shiver of her bottom as she climbed the high steps.

When they got back, and tumbled interlaced on to her bed, he noticed the staggered bookshelves, the room entirely insulated by the silence that books afford, and there were steps as though the components of his dream had been realized as a prop-arranged reality. He couldn't believe it, and Joanna's fingers were soon brushing the taut erection contained in his tight black jeans. Agonizingly ticklish impulses were travelling up and down his cock. And his hands were busy choreographing Joanna's body; he had her bra off and her top lifted, and his tongue moved in every variant route across her indigo nipples. He had her arch with pleasure as a foretaste of the passionate lovemaking to come.

He teased off her tights, but left the rest of her clothes intact as he was determined to have her act out the fantasy which had preoccupied him for such a period of time. Joanna was only too willing to comply with his suggestions, and tied her hair severely with a red ribbon, angled her St Laurent frames on the bridge of her nose, put her spike heels back on, positioned the steps and climbed provocatively towards the top shelf of her books, a collection she had been accumulating since childhood.

Greil stepped out of his shirt and jeans, and stood at the base of the steps. He looked right up her violet micro-skirt to the gusset of her black panties. Joanna took down a book, and according to plan began reading it. Greil was throbbing with anticipation. He took two steps up the ladder and hooked his thumbs into the elastic band of Joanna's panties, and then he began manoeuvring them centimetre by centimetre over her bottom, peeling them like the skin of an exotic fruit, and running a finger down the crack of her bottom. And he maintained this slow-motion action until her panties flopped at her ankles, and then he went back up the steps and tied her wrists with the flimsy black garment. He could see that Joanna was inordinately excited, and had never experienced anything like this inventive ritual. She was rotating her bottom in a circular arc as he began running his tongue up the backs of her legs, first the right and then the left leg, before making an exploratory reconnaissance of her pussy.

Joanna's silent gestures told Greil that she was pleading to be entered, but he delayed again and again, before finally pushing his tongue into her tight bud and hearing her voice issue a guttural commentary on his expertise. He then lifted her off the ladder, and placed her bottom up on the bed, and deliriously entered her to the hilt. He moved in and out of her with subtle and affirmative pressure, and felt her contract and release, contract and release until her orgasmic pitch reached an ecstatic shriek. Greil buried his cock in her as he came in a series of frenzied spasms.

They lay back on the bed, and he untied her wrists. He knew they would be urgent again in a short while, but for now they lay there talking of books, of Bowles, Burroughs and Genet, and of the whole spectrum of contemporary fiction, and Joanna licked her lips and ran a scarlet fingernail over page 93 of *Our Lady of the Flowers*.

Flying Kites

Roberta sat on the bed putting a gloss to her toenails. She had painted them co-ordinating colours, a black, a gold, a red, a green, and a silver on each foot. Her tiny feet looked like two fans which would have pleased a Chinese emperor in some autumnal dynasty when the foot was seen as the symbol of sex.

She was excited. For the past month, and throughout the blond heat of July, she had formed a liaison with a particular man, which was the more erotically charged by its remaining unsublimated. She had rented an apartment with a balcony overlooking the bushy end of the park. Each afternoon, her skin filmed with UV preparations, and sheltered by a floppy green umbrella, she sat on her terrace. She would read, listen to music and acquire a tan. As the place wasn't overlooked, she would bask topless in a string bikini bottom, or sometimes in nothing but the shiver of black chiffon panties. Roberta liked the erotic daring this challenge created, and it excited her to think that perhaps somewhere an eye was focused on her curves, an eye polishing itself on one of her splashy violet areolas.

It had begun like that. She had discovered in herself a repressed exhibitionist, and one afternoon she had stepped out to the balcony fully clothed and slowly with her back to the park, she had done a provocative strip-tease, all the while treating it as perfectly natural. She had slipped out of her top, and unfastened the back hook-and-eye catch of her black bra, and then imagining the increased excitement of someone watching her moves, she had unzipped her short floral skirt, and stood there with nothing but the dividing string of a black thong parting the compact curves of her bottom. And it was the day he first appeared. She had seen him out of the corner of her eye, the sort of man she had never known before. He was dressed in black trousers and a white frilly shirt, and was wearing light make-up. He just remained standing to the left of her vision, and she saw that he had been flying a pink kite which was shaped like an exotic fish. She thought of him as the Kite Man; he was gentle and in no way menacing, and they seemed to communicate without gestures. Roberta felt a sense of growing excitement in the young man's presence. It was as though he was directing an erotic beam at her, and she made no effort to conceal her breasts, but rather she sat there, legs arched in an acquiescent pose, inviting his attention. He stood for a long time looking directly at her, and then with the return of a light flurrying wind, he had relaunched his pink kite, and Roberta watched as their communion was choreographed on air waves above the trees.

When the young man disappeared, she was compelled to go indoors and excite herself. With the expertise of a gold-painted fingernail, she achieved intense orgasm thinking of the afternoon's encounter; when later that night her boyfriend came to the flat he found her waiting for him in nothing but a pair of pink transparent panties, and the passion she injected into lovemaking was fiercer than he had ever known. She had wanted him to do everything, and had surprised him with the dexterity of her tongue and fingers. But Roberta was disappointed that her boyfriend never noticed or commented on the little details, like how she had painted each toe and fingernail a different colour, and how she was wearing a perfume that was new for her, 1000 by Jean Patou, a heady, resonant scent which spoke of seduction; how she had tied her hair up in a black velvet band, and worn an anklet with *diamanté* sparkles in it – he had missed the things she knew the Kite Man would relish.

And she had played on him the tricks that men so often do to women, when they fantasize during sex that they're making love to a curvier female: she had brought the young man into her mind as Paul thrust so vigorously that the bed started to walk across the room, and when she had screamed out with pleasure it was the afternoon she was living out – the feelings of intense arousal the young man had transmitted to her body.

The next day, she spent a long time preparing herself to look beautiful for his arrival. She wore a shocking pink lipstick, let her luxurious black hair float loose, chose an emerald sequinned bikini bottom, and placed a gold chain round her waist. She looked like someone made up for a Helmut Newton shoot. Roberta knew that the young man would take in every feminine detail.

He appeared at exactly the same time as on the previous day. It was precisely 3.30. Roberta felt the rush of excitement in her abdomen as she stood leaning over the balcony and looking out across the park. She pretended not to have seen him, and turned round several times so that he could see how the emerald bikini fitted her bottom. She felt confident to flaunt herself in a way she would never have done with her boyfriend. She was discovering a vocabulary of sex in her gestures that had belonged previously to fantasy. She stood cupping her full breasts in her hands, and then with slow deliberately undulating movements, began applying oil to her body, running it in and around her nipples, extending the downward play of her hands to her navel, and then going back up again to her breasts. She was getting turned on by her sensuality. And every time she looked up, he was standing there watching, his pink kite at rest in the grass.

And again she experienced an amazing hum of energy in her erogenous zones. She was becoming freed of all inhibitions, and to test his responses she slipped a single finger into her elasticated bikini, one which had a black fingernail, and left it there. He came a little closer, and sat in the grass watching. Her impulse was to run a finger across her crotch; she was itching to be tickled between the legs. Instead she began studiously massaging the sole of her left foot, imparting, she hoped, an invitation for him to follow.

But he never moved. He watched her, and he kept his senses attuned to the wind. When the wind picked up a bit he launched his kite and with an expert hand navigated it above her balcony. The pink kite swam in the blue sky. And then Roberta realized he wanted her to catch it, and she held out her hand and got a firm hold of the line. It was her first contact with him, and although it was only a kite she stroked it as she might have done his body, exploring his chest, massaging his stomach, working a little finger across the outline of his cock until it triggered and demanded her whole hand to support its weight.

She noticed there was an envelope attached to the underside of the kite, and she knew instinctively it was intended for her to open. As she slipped the letter free, so he began to retrieve the kite, making it impossible for her to supply an answer to his note. When she opened the blue envelope, she thrilled at the contents of the message: 'I shall come here for thirteen days,' it said, 'and on the fourteenth we will make love. On that day I want you to wear for me whatever is most exotic in your wardrobe. I have fallen in love with you from a distance.'

And that night Roberta again gave Paul everything, for she fantasized about what it would be like in bed with the stranger on the fourteenth day. Paul couldn't understand Roberta's sudden increase in passion and her desire to experiment with new positions. He was frightened. He assumed that someone had been teaching her the things that he had never dared introduce into the bedroom. She now luxuriated in the 69 position, her tongue snaking up and down his length while she convulsed with climactic tension, and hungrily engorged him at the moment of his orgasm. Paul didn't dare question this lovemaking, but he was suspicious. He tried calling her at unusual hours, but she was always in, calm, and betrayed no guilt in her voice or signs that she was with a lover. On the contrary, she appeared surprised at the extra attention he was giving her personal life. But much to her disappointment, he still failed to notice her femininity; the things to which she had devoted such special attention seemed to mean nothing to him. Roberta wondered if Paul would ever perceive the mystique that surrounded a woman's body, and she suspected he wouldn't. Even though she attached much importance to little things in their foreplay, he gave no indication of having noticed. His obliviousness to her erotic signals made her lonely, and the volcanic lust that came alive in her at night and forced her body into the elastic positions of a dancer, was generated by her communications with the stranger in the afternoon, and had little to do with Paul's experimentation. Still, he was a good lover who would come two or three times in the course of their heated sessions, and Roberta was increasing her own knowledge of how to orgasm.

And so the meetings continued. Each afternoon she would dress for her visitor, and he would sit right below her balcony and commune with her that way. On the thirteenth afternoon she stepped out of a long black skirt and was wearing suspenders and stockings. She wondered that no one else came to this place which was notorious for lovers at night, but during the day remained deserted. She wanted to make love to him right there on her balcony, her legs wrapped round his back all through the lazy July afternoon. Each day the tempestuous desire to have physical contact with him increased, and each day he sent her a message via his pink kite. It was a sort of magic. She was spellbound, and he transmitted energies that flooded her mind with sexual imagery. The link between them was unbreakable. Sometimes when she thought of him she could have sworn flame crackled from her fingertips, and that her eyes changed from green to purple with passion.

When the fourteenth day came, it was just as she had expected. The sun was up, a light breeze shivered in the plane trees, and she felt fired up with passion. She spent from noon onwards preparing herself. She took a bath scented with lavender, plum and ylang-ylang, repainted her nails in individually enamouring colours, spent a long time on her make-up, chose a pair of the wispiest green transparent panties, wrote the words

I LOVE YOU in red lipstick on her bottom, put on a black sequinned micro-skirt with a green chiffon top, and awaited her lover, for she had come to think of him as that. And he was there in his usual place, playing a kite into the trees and clearly awaiting her arrival. She stood there looking the perfect accompaniment to his elegance, he was once again in his white frilly shirt and black trousers, and was wearing a sparkling brooch pinned to a black beret. This time Roberta kept her clothes on, for she wanted the stranger to undress her in the intimacy of the bedroom. Her skirt was so short it revealed almost everything, but preserved the little mysteries that he would soon make his own. And anyhow she felt his eyes could see right through her clothes. He had that sort of magic.

She blew him a kiss that opened like a rose on her lips. He could taste the scent of her lipstick from his spot on the grass. He walked over to a tree and stood with his back to it and looked full at her, and then he walked straight towards her, his kite over his shoulder. She signalled to him that the door was open, and she waited out on the balcony, determined that their passion should start there, before progressing to the bedroom.

And he was just as she had expected. His blue eyes were like bits of the sky, his mouth tasted of the accumulated heat of July days spent outside, his body was sinuous and charged with erotic tension. She pulled him down on to cushions, and his hands quickly had her out of her skirt and chiffon top. She could no longer think, and surrendered to him totally. And when he picked her up to carry her indoors to the bedroom with its curtains already drawn, she could see that there was someone watching in the trees. It was only an ordinary voyeur, but it excited her to know that someone else knew what they were about to do. And who knows, Roberta surprised herself thinking, perhaps in time he too would court her in a ritualistic way, and become her new lover.

Blue Bra Straps in a Bookstore

Ruby put on a cassette of Billie Holiday and settled to the mid-afternoon vacuum in the secondhand bookshop. Billie's voice sounded like a blue Sunday afternoon, when there's nothing to do but walk round the docks dreaming of a lost love in Paris, and of a future the mauve of lilacs, the mauve of a rainbow. The voice covered the whole gamut of inconsolable pain, and of singing to pay for the next desperate fix. Lady Day had become an icon for those who celebrated loneliness within love.

Ruby had a pile of secondhand fiction to mark up, and she busied herself checking first editions from reprints, novels in dust-jackets from those without, a nice copy of André Gide's *Strait is the Gate*, a valuable first of J. G. Ballard's *The Atrocity Exhibition*, and an undistinguished edition of *En Ménage*, Huysmans's novel about *fin-de-siècle* French prostitutes.

When she looked up, he was browsing in the fiction section. She had seen him in the shop often, and remained insatiably curious about his remoteness, the fineness of his aesthetic features, and the aura of mystery attached to his person. She had heard that he was a cult writer with a small but fanatical following. His books fell into a decadent tradition and incorporated surreal, sci-fi and futuristic imaginings. He looked like someone who didn't really belong to the insurgent crowds down Charing Cross Road. To Ruby he was clearly an Aquarian, and someone who was looking out for his future species to arrive. He could have been bisexual, but on one occasion she had watched his eye trapped on her shoulder, conscious that her dark blue bra strap had snaked free from her top and was visibly, suggestively in his line of vision. She had the hunch that he desired her, but he looked incommunicatively introspective, and she sensed it would take just the right combination of felicitous events before he approached her directly as a person, and not an assistant.

Ruby was glad she had touched up her lipstick, its scarlet gloss standing out in contrast to her pale face and green eyes. She was wearing a skimpy green top designed to show off her midriff, and tight blue jeans which mapped out the contours of her curves like a second skin. She was a quiet girl who had known love and the bitterness of its going wrong, and who preferred to take refuge in the imagination rather than settle for the wrong partner. She was a dreamer, who punctuated her life amongst books with intermittent forays to clubs, although her love/hate attraction to the latter was inspired more by the wish to dress up outrageously than to immerse herself fully in an atmosphere of noise and claustrophobic pressure. Like all shy people, Ruby nurtured the repressed ostentation of a glam diva.

She looked across at his slim figure. His eyes and fingers were busy at work on a line of shelf novels, and she noticed the way his touch choreographed rather than handled the books which aroused his curiosity. Ruby was hoping he would come up with items of interest, for then she would have the chance to engage him in conversation at the till. She knew she was looking good today, and her electric charge was up and affording her confidence.

Billie's voice continued to infiltrate the shop, the death-wish implied by 'Gloomy Sunday' seeming to create a black rainbow indoors. She knew he would be listening, as he riffled the books in the poetry section, extracting one or two volumes and placing them together with others in his left hand, while with his right he continued to browse. He was dressed in black and white. A white cotton shirt, and black trousers. Usually he wore a sparkling brooch somewhere on his clothes, and this time she could see that the glitter on him was in the form of a single drop earring which flashed in his hair.

Ruby felt unnaturally anticipative and excited. She noticed how without any fabrication both her bra straps were visible again, as though his presence excited this state of *déshabillé*. She let it go, realizing that the little hints of blue-black were a glamorous flourish to her appearance. She would appear just a little provocative in his eyes.

She found it hard to concentrate on her task, particularly as he had moved over to the erotic section and was assiduously preoccupied with a book he appeared to be tasting at leisure. She could see that he was far away with the text, and that his blue eyes had entered another dimension of reality. Ruby was hoping that he would purchase this book, for it would offer her another clue as to the geography of his mind.

It was raining outside. It was her private belief that playing Billie Holiday invited rain, and the abrupt shower rapped on the shop window with glass knuckles. With no customers other than the solitary young man who had been attracting her attention for months, and with Billie Holiday's voice orchestrating the fast London rain, the shop seemed to Ruby like an intimate recess designed to bring about their meeting.

Having finished pricing the books piled on the counter, Ruby went over to the fiction section to place the books in alphabetical order on the shelves. She had kicked off her shoes and was conscious of the way her jeans created a provocatively constricted walk. Two weeks ago she had sewn a scarlet love-heart logo on one of the back pockets, and she imagined his eye focusing on it as she climbed the steps to a high shelf. She tried to act unselfconsciously, and once on glancing down she could see that his concentration hadn't shifted from the erotic book he was busy perusing.

Or had it? She couldn't be sure. His movements were always understated and on the edge of being retrieved. Ruby walked over to the relevant sections to place books, and then crossed the shop and looked out at the scintillating torrent as it drummed across the traffic and the streets. Pedestrians were racing for cover. A black cab was sheeted in prismatic crystals. And Billie Holiday kept on singing across a quirky sax and orchestra. The whole band sounded like they were playing on a ship's deck in perilous seas.

Ruby ran her hands over her round bottom packed into tight denims. She felt particularly sensual, and savoured the moment of running her tongue across her perfumed Dior lipstick. A lover in Paris had once told her that Dior lipsticks tasted of aphrodisiacal aniseed. She wondered how the young man still browsing in the erotic section would respond to the flavour of her ultra-scarlet gloss. There was no let-up in the rain, the sky was an inky purple over Leicester Square, and the summer shower thundered across the West End. There were Chinese girls opposite running for cover into a supermarket hall. The traffic had stalled to a collectively irate hum.

Ruby went back and sat by the till and followed Billie Holiday's blue tangent of broken-hearted reverie. There wasn't much to do but sit and wait for the young man to come over to the counter and pay for his increasing pile of books. She had been shy in the past, but with both her bra straps showing she was determined to engage him in some sort of personal conversation. She had decided she really fancied him, and felt desperate that this could be the last time he would visit the shop. What if he were to disappear for an extended holiday? What if a lover called him across the seas to a foreign country? Ruby ran over the inventory of possibilities in her mind. And the rain kept on throwing itself at the window, as though someone was hammering tacks into a carpet.

He was still squatting down, paying particular attention to the erotic fiction. She hoped he would come across to the counter soon for she feared new customers would in time intrude on what she had established in her mind as their privacy.

She could feel his concentration break, and he stood up abruptly, scanned a last shelf and made his way over to the counter. He was even more beautiful than she had imagined, his lips were full and sensual, and he wore a tiny diamond chip implanted in his left nostril. Ruby was suddenly conscious of her own charms, her tanned waist, her pronounced breasts, the projection of her hipbones. And almost without being responsible for saying it, she said, 'I've noticed you here before, I wish you came in more often.'

He smiled, but was evidently shy. He placed his books down on the counter, and said to her, 'I'm Sebastian. I write novels of a particularly weird nature, and I live in the Covent Garden area. I'm often invisible for weeks, and then I come out to buy books.'

Ruby looked at his pile of purchases. He had chosen a copy of Anaïs Nin's *Delta of Venus*, a number of books of poetry including John Ashbery's *Selected Poems*; at the bottom of the pile was a copy of *Irene*, the pornographic French novel which went under the name of Albert de Routisie, although true authorship was debated, and not properly known. Ruby had glanced into this book while shelving it a week ago, and had opened at the passage where the overexcited client shoots his sperm between the eyes of the prostitute who is intent on giving him head. She couldn't forget the details, and now tried to imagine the young man's solitary excitement when he came to read passages like this one. Maybe he wasn't as shy as he made out, she found herself speculating. Perhaps at this very moment he was imagining what it would be like to unclip her cobalt bra and begin circling her nipples with his lips. She couldn't tell.

They stood there, she thumbing through the prices, hoping time would expand, and that a date would ensue from this meeting, and he placing his eyes on her in a way that reminded her of pinning jewellery to a jumper or a coat. His eyes seemed to tickle her although she knew she was imagining it. And Billie Holiday was singing 'I Cover the Waterfront', as the rain began to let up, and a dazzle of light jumped into the shop from the brighter sky.

'I like your selection of books,' Ruby ventured. 'They're my sort of reading. In fact I've dipped into one or two of these, while they've been dormant on the shelves. *Irene* is quite a scarce book.'

She could feel his eyes beginning to leave sun-spots on her navel. It was like those green irises left singe-marks on her satin skin. His eyes caressed her like a lover's fingertips, and she could feel them everywhere. They left a prickling sensation on her bottom, they got trapped in the sensitive spots on her shoulders. It felt like she had him in her arms, intimately, fluently, and that he was surprising her with his adventurous caresses. She had known men explore her body like a preconceived map, and others who had discovered places she hadn't realized were a part of her. Sebastian was definitely of the latter kind. He was finding nerve points in her that lit up like constellations. She knew that if she got this man into bed he would prove the most explorative of lovers. And already he was making love to her by eye contact.

'It all adds up to forty pounds,' she heard herself saying, as she jumped back to the reality of the situation, implanting in her mind the truth that he was the customer and she the assistant. Billie's voice was turning a deeper shade of blue in the background. It was the blue of gentians and delphiniums. Time and the London crowds had started up again, and Ruby could feel the outside world breaking into the inviolable interlude they had established. She was desperate to establish a deeper connection with this young man, and suddenly and without her expressing the least surprise or resistance, he placed a tentative left hand on her right shoulder, and while he spoke to her of books, played with her blue bra strap as an indication of how he would slowly undress her. The gesture was playful but intended in its resolve. And Ruby kept thinking that she had never let a stranger make snapping sounds with her bra strap, or ever would allow one that liberty. This was an exception, and she found it hard to believe in the reality of the situation. It was all so sudden and yet it felt like he had made love to her through this intimate gesture.

'I could meet you tonight,' he said, 'if you haven't got other plans. Seven o'clock outside Covent Garden tube station?'

'I'll be there,' Ruby replied, without mentally daring to consult a prior engagement. She felt up-ended, and adrenalin rushed through her body. There were only three hours to wait. Sebastian left as mysteriously as he had entered. Ruby covered up her blue bra straps. Two customers had entered the shop, and she settled to the circumspect occupation of pricing. Her body felt like it was lit with stars. She knew tonight they would really blaze.

Lima Blues (after Anaïs Nin's 'Mathilde')

Mathilde was a hat maker in Paris, and she worked from home in a basement that her clients visited. Her diffidence, perfect figure, violet eyes, and the long line of her seamed stockinged legs, made her instantly attractive to her male clients. Those who had come to her to buy hats for their wives or girlfriends invariably attempted to touch her, or insidiously and persistently tried to look up her skirt. It was a sensitive situation. Mathilde would be reaching to take a hat out of its protective tissue, and to place it on a stand, and she would feel a finger trace the defined crack of her bottom through tight jeans, or a still tighter skirt, or a hand would reach round and cup a pronounced breast in a sensually affirmative grip. And the women were sometimes no better. One of her regular clients, a singer called Evangeline, had dared slip a hand up the back of Mathilde's micro-mini, and had quickly inserted a finger beneath her black panties.

These were the embarrassments that Mathilde incurred as a devastatingly attractive woman working from home. And no one ever bothered to ask her if she was single, or lonely, or even remotely interested in a date. They assumed that for the space of time in which they were in the shop, her body was conquerable, and her mind manipulable. And of course the nature of her work with fabrics was sensual, intimate, and inspired in her the wish to find a man distinguished by poetic eloquence and a romantic heart.

Mathilde heightened her attractiveness by resistance. The word had got out that she was unavailable, but that she wouldn't reproach those who made flirtatious advances. And for men who received gratification through a woman's indifference, Mathilde seemed the ideal partner. There was one man, a particularly rich and appreciative customer, who tirelessly bought new and bizarre creations for his wife, who had on one occasion unzipped, taken his cock out, and at a strategic point when she was bending over in a skirt that seemed sewn to her bottom, had mounted her from behind and come all over her skirt. Nothing had been said by either person, but Mathilde in a state of disgust had thrown the garment away, not even wishing to send it to the cleaners.

And there was the incident with the schoolboys who had wanted to discover what colour panties she was wearing under a pleated mini, and one of them had devised an elaborate story about wishing to purchase a hat for his mother's birthday, and with her back turned, and straining up to lift a blue construct from a stand, the boy had darted forward, lifted up her skirt, and then to a collective cry of 'Black!', had with his other friends run madly out of the shop, leaving Mathilde with the unwelcome reflection that her preference for tiny black panties would soon be known all over the neighbourhood. She imagined the boys feverishly wanking over what they had seen, and comparing their impressions of how tightly the black silk was moulded to her buttocks.

It was when the Baron had told her that French women were highly prized in South America, because of their expertise in lovemaking, their pale skin, their vivacity, and their intelligence, that Mathilde had felt compelled to change her life for a time, and to go and live in Lima. It would be an experiment, and if it failed, she would return to her old life in Paris. The Baron was a peculiar one. He had once paid her double the price for an expensive cerise silk beret, had immediately taken it out of the black tissue paper in which she had wrapped it, had produced an unsparing erection and spent the next four or five minutes convulsively masturbating into the silk beret, before discarding the stained cerise fetish in her wastebin, and without a word of explanation exiting from the shop. It was a procedure he had repeated on three other occasions, once in a mauve turban generously sprinkled with pearls, another time in a balaclava, squeezing his last drop out with vociferous satisfaction, and a third time in a leopard-spotted fedora, his left hand clamping the hat over his penis, while his right worked with a terrifying rhythm towards climax.

Mathilde had wondered why she took these perverse demonstrations of sexuality so passively. Did all men jerk off into designer hats, she wondered, were her expert creations worth so little that her violet and scarlet silk linings had immediately to be defaced by scalding jism? Of course the hats were substitutes for her pussy, but Mathilde was adamant that she would never give herself to the wrong man.

Even the flight to Lima had involved her in a quasi-sexual experience. She had found herself sitting next to a man with obvious aesthetic leanings; his long tapered fingers, transparent green eyes, and black cashmere suit had impressed on her his manifestly refined sensibility. They had begun talking, as is the way in the apprehensive excitement of transatlantic flights, and somehow, after considerable circumventions of the topic, the man (called Antoine) had arrived at the confessional secret he shouldn't tell her, didn't dare to tell her, but anyhow would. It turned out (with some embarrassment on his part) that he was the mind behind manufacturing latex sex dolls, or rather the most advanced life-like dolls, custom-made to the client's desired statistics, a Lolita, a Bardot, a Monroe, according to preference. A sixteen-year-old Chinese virgin, or the voluptuous proportions of a Spanish courtesan. Mathilde listened to Antoine relate the story of how he was no longer able to make love to either women or men – he had owned to propensities for both – and was now able to achieve sexual pleasure only through dolls. He was, he confessed, turned on by the tactile qualities of lubricated latex. He dared advance to Mathilde that he used the anal aperture exclusively, for he preferred the constricted fit. He had had a doll made for him which was hermaphroditic: it had a penis, vagina, and breasts, and of course the snug anal aperture.

Antoine spoke of this particular doll with rapture. It was his idea of total erotic fulfilment, and although he informed Mathilde that such bodies were to be found on the streets of Paris, Rome, and Rio, he felt better accommodated by a latex version which would adopt whatever fetish he intended for a particular session. Even talking of the subject excited him, and Mathilde knew from the man's watery green eyes that he was stiff as he spoke to her, and that he was re-enacting erotic pleasures in his mind. 'This one's on board,' he confided, 'I call him or her Lauren. The flight crew would die if they knew she was eagerly awaiting me in an olive-coloured suitcase. Tonight I will be locked in Lauren's elastic embrace, cock up one passage, and a finger up the other.'

Mathilde found Antoine's lurid descriptions of unilateral sex both repulsive and exciting. She was suddenly aware that her short black skirt, worn to match a suit jacket, was riding high, almost to her crotch, and for a moment she thought that yet another person was going to know of her preference for tiny black knickers. She corrected the potential danger, but felt moist, and her pulse was running away with a percussive beat. They were an hour from landing, and Mathilde kept hoping that Antoine would place a hand on her transparent thigh, for she was wearing silk stockings, and her skirt was too impossibly short to keep from riding up to the dark stocking tops, taut black suspender straps holding them in place. She had spent her life resisting the illicit advances made to her in her Paris basement, but she would have made an exception for this unusual man, and as she was wearing stockings and not tights, his finger would have immediate access to the gusset of her black panties. But Antoine was clearly too removed from the idea of a physical body to advance the caress that so many men would have offered in his place.

In Lima, Mathilde viewed the men as invested with the romantic ideals and natural poetic eloquence that she had failed to find in their Parisian counterparts. She found herself rapidly descending into low-life. She took a small shop in the red-light district, and one day she stood in the window naked, dressed in nothing but a pair of scarlet stilettos. She spent a long time dressing the window, and placing exotically styled hats on the various mannequins. At other times she would be topless as she served customers, her only protection against their eyes being a high-cut black tanga brief. She had earned the reputation of being the untouchable one, and it annoyed and frustrated her that she had taken the image to such extremes, and that it had come to be accepted by her male clients that they shouldn't pinch or slap her bottom, or in any way make designs on her body.

In the evenings she would visit opium dens, and artists' lofts, and lie on mattresses and smoke until all her sensations were heightened to the point of overload. If there was a couple petting or fucking on another mattress, she would indirectly experience both their pleasures, the delayed orgasm that the man achieved after making love to the woman in slow motion over a number of hours, and the magnified pleasure of her experiencing every thrust like a multiple orgasm. Their sensual thrills travelled through Mathilde's body like a form of osmotic telepathy, and sometimes she found herself coming without using her fingers or drawing any attention to the fact she was finding prolonged release through orgasm. Her face portrayed not the least ripple of pleasure as she underwent the slow build-up to a deliciously sustained crisis. She watched the dark-bodied woman on the couch with an art student arch her hips as she built to orgasm, kick her legs up high in a half somersault and emit a convulsive shriek as pleasure tore through her body again and again.

Sometimes there were geometric orgies involving several couples, and one woman was being fed a penis into her mouth while she lay on top of a man who was fucking her, and another man was simultaneously having her up the back passage, while his balls were being licked by a Spanish girl called Anna, whose gold hooped earrings tinkled with the oscillating movements of her head as she worked dexterously at the man's enflamed scrotum. No one ever suggested that Mathilde should join in the fun, or tried to lead her by the hand to a bed, or attempted to take one of her violet nipples between his forefinger and thumb. She was left alone to lose herself in sensual reverie, and to undergo the permutations of image induced by the drug, which made her feel that she was watching a film inside her head.

Sometimes, Mathilde would go and sit in front of a large mirror in the corner of the room and just stare at herself. She had dyed her pubic hair blue, and the curiosity that her triangle aroused in her own eyes seemed to demand no immediate attention from the others. They were lost in their pipes, or distracted by staring at a beauty-spot on a buttock, or dotted just above a lip or nipple. Mathilde filled in her own time with abstract reflection, but often went home at dawn with a feeling of sexual relief. She had come indirectly and through arousal generated by watching a woman undergoing protracted cunnilingus. The man would lap the woman like a cat its milk.

Now and then she would think of Antoine. She hoped she would meet him again in the city, and she knew instinctually that she would give herself to him like she had never before offered herself to a man.

Business flourished. She produced extraordinary creations for prostitutes and local beauties, and there was a generous transsexual clientele, who brought her outrageous drawings of the ostentatious designs they wished to have made. One of them wanted a black felt hat shaped like an erect penis, with a ruby for an eye, and the word death embroidered on the base in pearls to symbolize her being an artificially created woman without the encumbrance of a cock. The hat had to be made according to the size of the transsexual's severed penis, for he had paid a taxidermist to preserve his genitalia. Mathilde was open to anything. She fashioned hats that looked like roses, seashells, UFOs, and any number of elaborate French pastries.

And sometimes she worked in transparent bodies, bikinis, fishnet lingerie, and once in open-crotch black panties, but still no one dared to touch her, or even ask her out. Her reputation as inviolable and invincible had strengthened independently of her, and she began to wonder if she was under a spell, or had been cursed by a local witch. At night she would lie on her bed, legs interminably open, and give herself the attention that men so assiduously denied her. Her bed would rattle and creak with her efforts, and an ear trained to the wall would have assumed that she had an eager lover who was riding her with the persistence of a stud. Her bed would squeak periodically until dawn, and in the morning she would appear with mauve rings around her eyes, and an expression of jaded sensuality on her lips.

It occurred to her that perhaps word was out that she was married, or entertained a secret lover at night, one whose sexual drive was indomitably obstinate. It occurred to her that men might be apprehensive that they would not live up to her insatiable demand for erotic torment. And the days hurried by with her vivaciously enthusiastic clients at the shop, and her occasional visits to opium dens at night, or to brothels in which she would pay to observe couples through a system of two-way mirrors.

One day Antoine came into her shop, looking coolly debonair and sartorially correct. She shut the door and the blinds after him, and served him tea, and was glad that she was a little more formally dressed in her green top and a tight black mini. He was carrying a valise, and she imagined the intersexual doll was inside and conveniently deflated. But this time Antoine was visibly interested in her, and as Mathilde strained to reach for a number of boxes up high, so he let his hand trace the curve of her bottom and come to rest at the point where back meets front. His finger lingered there, and Mathilde felt herself flush moist. She wanted this man to lay her catastrophically, and to fuck her so hard that all her sexual frustration over the years would find incandescent release in orgasm.

Mathilde turned around and fitted her mouth over Antoine's like a sweet poison, and for him it was like rolling his tongue into a ruby pomegranate as he reciprocated her passion. His hands were soon alerted to her erect nipples, and were busy lifting the back of her short skirt, as he fitted his thumbs into the elastic of her minimal panties. 'This has got to be special,' Antoine whispered into her ear, and she led him up the stairs to her bedroom above the shop, and as she did so, her movements constricted by the tightness of her pinched skirt, she felt like a tart leading a client to her room. She thought of the old Cole Porter lyrics: 'If you want to buy my wares/Follow me and climb the stairs', and sang these lines to herself as Antoine followed her into a bedroom all done out in black and purple drapes, with the bed curtained off by chiffon hangings.

Mathilde undressed, and wriggled into a bottom-up position on the bed. She could hear Antoine unpack his valise, and impatient for him to join her in an accommodating 69 position, she heard not deep breathing, but the sound of the doll being inflated. 'I need you both together,' Antoine whispered. 'It's my only way to get back to the flesh. Simultaneous lovemaking.' His adroitness made Mathilde realize he must have planned the incident to the last detail; he mounted the doll on Mathilde's arched back, so that its bottom came to rest at the same level as her own, and with an invigorating thrust he entered her pussy from behind, and positioned himself deep within her, while correspondingly licking the latex pussy of the doll he steadied in place above Mathilde's own bottom.

Mathilde surrendered herself to the weird act of dual sex, and after so many years of self-induced pleasure felt the orgasm build with cataclysmic pressure inside her. It must have been thundering outside, she could hear pianos being thrown around in the clouds, and rain swiping the hot streets, and Antoine straining to please the surreal artefact of a double pussy.

Lana's Adventure

They decided on London. An hour's flight from Amsterdam found them in a city climatically the same, but with weird energy lines buzzing through the grey uniformity of the crowds. They hopped from zone to zone in the back of black cabs, and enjoyed the notion of being secretly cut off from the world, as though they had exchanged one hotel room for another. And it was during these short rides with Marco that Lana started to conceive the fantasy of wearing nothing but black silk panties under her long leopard-skin coat, and of enticing her boyfriend to commit surreptitious acts under that coat, perhaps resulting in full consummation as the taxi wavered on an endless circuit through the city's wastelands. Lana knew that cabbies would accept payment for hiring a taxi for sex.

But on this ride from Chelsea to the West End, she was dressed under her spectacular coat in a violet mini-skirt, knee-high black suede boots and fish-net tights. She pressed herself up to Marco, took his hand and placed it on her knee. Her coat was open, and she could imagine the driver was following the fish-net curve of her thighs in his mirror. She toyed with Marco's hand, playfully extending it further to her thighs, and working her pink Dior lips into the helix of his ear. She could feel the tension at his denimed crotch, the fabric straining as his erection quickened. Just three hours ago, on immediate arrival at their Kensington hotel, they had made convulsive love. They were both excited by the comfort and anonymity of their bedroom. They had tumbled on to the bed, her skirt riding up to her hips, and without even undressing her Marco had laid her with the ferocity of a panther falling on its prey. As she had built rapidly towards orgasm, she had instructed him to tear the panties off her bottom as she was coming. And he had shredded the fabric with alacrity, his fingernails acting like claws, the tearing sound heightening the pleasure for both of them, as climax subsided in a scale of expiring obscenities.

They knew that by the time they returned to the hotel, they would be itching for more. Hotels always drove them to bursts of perverse erotomania. Lana wanted to heighten that eventual lovemaking by letting Marco know that he could take liberties with her at any time during their London stay.

'Darling, I'm feeling so ticklish,' she whispered in his ear. 'Let's see how the driver responds when he knows you're tickling my pussy.'

Marco, who was by nature taciturn and discreet, didn't need much encouragement. He found himself willingly acting out of role, and began to kiss her deeply and passionately, his hand slipping beneath her little mauve skirt. And without any attempt to disguise his action, Lana opened her legs so as to make it easy for him to begin a one-fingered sensual exploration of her clitoris. And she really was excited. The motion of the taxi as it rocked over inconsistencies in the road surface, the abrupt acceleration away from lights, or the car's sitting immobile in the traffic for long periods, all of these things assisted the excitement she felt at Marco's adventurous finger.

'I bet he's bursting in his pants,' Marco whispered, referring to the cabbie, who must have been watching their petting in the driver's mirror. Marco too was beginning to find the game unnaturally stimulating, and Lana wasn't surprised when he guided her hand towards his zip, and said, 'Darling, tickle me, run your nails up and down my length.'

Lana dipped into Marco's open zip, using, like him, one finger to excite response. She could feel his eight-inch throbbing penis trigger almost to the height of his belly button. Nothing was visible, but to a voyeuristic eye, the tension was increased by the idea of concealment.

'Do you want me to drive you round all afternoon?' the driver said impatiently, a note of frustration in his voice.

'No, stop just here, please,' Lana said, bundling Marco out of the taxi, and instantly flagging down another cab so that they could resume their petting.

'We want to drive round Docklands and the old parts of the city,' she informed the new driver, and then as abruptly closed the sliding partition. They were both eager to continue their sexual adventure. They intended to excite each other to a degree of intensity that would end in their having a taxi take them back to the hotel where the final consummation would take place.

'I've always wanted to be in just my lingerie under a long coat,' Lana whispered to Marco as they resumed kissing. And this time he began stroking her breasts. He pulled her coat off the shoulders so that the driver could see her large conical breasts standing out through the thin fabric of a blouse. He began caressing them from the outside, then with meticulous attention to detail he popped one button open at the waist, then another and another, until her black lace bra was visible. He then began licking her cleavage and placing impassioned kisses on her breasts. All the while she placed her arms round his neck and whispered enticements to go slower, further, and then to unclip her bra. Before he did so, they looked up and they could see the driver fumbling with his trousers, as though his erection had got trapped, and needed to be lifted from constraint. They could sense the man was excited by what he could see, and Lana giggled as Marco pushed her lace bra down and began circling her nipples with his tongue. She burnt with excitement. He had never shown greater delicacy, and the need for relative caution made him more attentive to little things that he might otherwise have rushed. Their taxi rides were turning into bouts of deliciously extended foreplay. Marco had never kissed her breasts for so long, and she thrilled to the sensation of having his hot lips dab at her areolas. She had to resist the temptation to place her own hand between her legs and uncontrollably frig herself off to the accompaniment of his caresses. He had both of her breasts jutting out from her coat, and twice when she looked up at a pause in the traffic flow, she could see drivers on each side making big-eyed indulgent gestures at her escaped tits. She stuck her tongue out between her red lips as a gesture of provocative defiance to one particularly demonstrative driver, and then resumed kissing Marco.

'In the next taxi, I want you to take my skirt off,' she said. 'But for now, tickle me everywhere. I'm red hot for your fingers.'

London was passing them by without their showing the least interest in their surroundings. The taxi was somewhere in the City, cruising the river, and the driver pushed back the glass and said, 'Do you want to stop off at a riverside pub?'

'No thanks,' Lana called back, 'we're busy.' Lana couldn't have enough of Marco's kisses on her shoulder and breasts. She was purring under his sensual advances. He was also placing kisses on her stomach, and already she was anticipating how in the next taxi, or the ride after that, his lips would be on her pussy, or would it be she who gave him head as the taxi drove along the Mall?

As a means of keeping them both in suspense, she asked the driver to stop, and as on the previous occasion they quickly exchanged one cab for another. Lana had placed her bra in a carrier, and had every intention that her skirt would also end up in that receptacle.

'Just drive round central London,' she told the driver, before sticking her tongue in Marco's ear. 'Anywhere is fine, we're too busy to care.'

Lana was thrilled by her newly discovered audacity. And Marco immediately pulled her coat open and placed his hand under her skirt. They could see the driver was wide-eyed and heated at the sight of Lana's long fish-net legs extending from a skirt no wider than a belt. The man hadn't counted on this sort of voyeuristic entertainment in the middle of the afternoon.

'Why don't you bring me right out,' Marco pleaded. 'Let

him see it. I'm as hard as a tent pole, and I've a good mind to have you sit on me while we fuck.'

'Not so quick, darling,' Lana smooched, 'I want this foreplay to go on all afternoon. But why don't you try taking off my skirt? You know where to find the zip. It's at the back.'

The taxi chugged into dilatory traffic. For a long time the car was hardly moving, and when it went forward it was only for a few seconds at a time. Marco was slowly, very slowly undoing Lana's zip. The electric crackle of Lana unzipping a skirt had never failed to excite him, and now he went about things precisely, creating and recreating the sound to stimulate them both, sliding the zip down and then drawing it up again, so that his penis was orchestrated into excitement by this intimate sound. When he took her skirt off it was by fractions, easing it slowly down past her bottom, and even more slowly towards her thighs, knowing the whole time that the driver was watching them. The tiny violet skirt began a descent to Lana's knees, and she placed her red fingernails on either side of Marco's face as he performed this seductive rolling. He pushed the skirt over her knees, and continued the move downwards. He got it to the calves of her legs, and by its own momentum it dropped to her ankles, and stayed there like a violet border over her black pointed boots.

The driver would know now that she was in her lingerie under the leopard-skin coat. The thought of this incited them to be more daring, and Lana sat on Marco's lap so that he could feel her bottom pivoting on his erection. Her movements simulated the act of making love, as she wriggled around on him, her tongue running from his neck to his shoulder. It was now her turn to undo his shirt buttons, and soon his chest was naked beneath his black jacket. Lana began applying big splashy kisses to the exposed areas of Marco's torso. Her red lipstick left roses on his nipples. It was all he could do to prevent himself from coming, particularly when her fingers began to run up and down the shaft of his cock again. He was aching to have her lips close over him and administer head.

'I want to slip my tights off,' she said, but to do this she had first to remove her boots. The driver was flushed as she removed one knee-high boot and then the other, rolled down her fishnet tights, and bunched them off. She then replaced her boots with studied movements, and drew the coat over her thighs so the driver couldn't see her black silk panties. Lana was getting high on her immodesty – never in her life had she been a sexual exhibitionist, and she and Marco were both discovering a penchant to shock the spectator. She had often felt turned on by the sight of couples petting in their local park, and at such times had pulled Marco down to her with a desperate urgency, but she had never presumed that she would end as a half-dressed woman in the back of a black cab, instructing the driver to take them anywhere.

'Lick me,' she instructed him, 'but get there slowly,' and soon he was crouched down on the floor, his tongue travelling the length of her thighs and stopping just short of her crotch. The driver was becoming visibly disconcerted.

'Do you want me to park up someplace, and go off to the pub?' he asked.

'We're far too busy for that,' said Lana, her head thrown back against the seat, her mouth starting to pout open as Marco's tongue flickered across the ridge of her wet panties. She wanted to guide him, and took hold of the back of his head in order to slow his urgency. 'Take all day,' she said, 'I've just seen Trafalgar Square, and I'm in ecstasy....'

Marco had never conceived that he would give perfect cunnilingus to Lana in the back of a taxi, while the car negotiated a traffic slick leading to the Haymarket. He had never enjoyed sex so much. Lana's pussy tasted better than a June strawberry. It was intoxicatingly spiced with love juices. His tongue had found the hood of her clit and was kneading it with a tantalizing sensitivity. Lana was beginning to moan. The driver said nothing. He slogged the car into traffic lanes, opening up when the road permitted. Lana couldn't repress the orgasm that was building. She could feel the convulsive tension mount in her pelvis. And then it was happening, spreading through her like a current, and she bit her lip to prevent from shrieking. She knew that this was the first of a chain of clitoral orgasms she was going to receive before they returned to the hotel for intense lovemaking.

'It's my turn now,' she said, wrapping the leopard-skin coat round her, and going down on the floor in a kneeling position. She coaxed his penis out and began licking it like an ice-lolly. She nibbled, pecked, and drew back from her handiwork. She liked to see his skin glisten with her saliva. For good measure she placed a red lipstick bite on the tip, and then returned to playing with it with her tongue. She wanted to prevent him from coming, so she wouldn't swallow on it. She refused to deep-throat his quivering shaft. Instead, she played with it like a cat. She prodded it with her tongue, and cushioned the head on her lips. She cradled him with her warmth, her mouth closing over him gently like a carnation.

'Don't come in the taxi,' she said. 'We don't want to give the driver that pleasure. Once we're back at the hotel, you'll fuck me crazily. I'm so hot for it I could scream. Let's do one more round of the sights, and get the taxi in the direction of the hotel.'

'Take us once round the West End, then back to Kensington,' she instructed the driver. The man was angling himself so he could see every detail of their explicit petting. Neither of them had ever felt so unashamedly uninhibited in their lives. They took in brief flashes of London, a line of shops, the dense trees skirting a park, the crowds hurrying across the road, the sudden shower flashing across the façades of buildings in a detonative burst. There were inky black clouds rolling across a stormy blue sky.

Now they were headed west towards Hyde Park and Notting Hill Gate. Lana zipped Marco up, despite his pleading for more, and placed his left hand under the divide of her coat. 'Carry on tickling me,' she said. 'All the way to the hotel.' And Marco applied a pianistic delicacy in enlarging Lana's clit to the size of a mauve fuchsia bud. It was like her whole body depended on his finger, for all of her was contracted into that one burning centre. He could hear from her suppressed cries that she was nearing another orgasm. A light flickered across his closed eyes. When he blinked clear he could see a blue-black sky zigzagged with spirals of lightning. A snappy electric storm was smashing across the blue cupola of the city sky. A few seconds later, the rain arrived. Crystal pendants fizzed across the taxi's metallic shell. It was a torrent of scintillating earrings rapping on the convex roof. A staccato excitation to lust.

Marco hung on to Lana's lips like a bee. Static was charging everything. The driver brought the car to a halt in the dazzle escaped from the sky. They could hear irate horns sounding through the impressive rain. It was like sitting in an igloo. It encouraged them to greater liberties. Marco's finger, which touched Lana with the delicacy of someone dusting an eyelid, found a reciprocal response in her touch. They were in perfect unison, their nerves excited to a corresponding pitch.

Cars slewed across the road. Thunder reverberated on the skyline. They were sealed in by their own breath and the rain. It was like thousands of silver tadpoles were wriggling on the glass. The taxi was brought to a complete halt. Somewhere behind them they could hear the sirens of emergency services attempting to open up a gap in the dead maze of traffic. Another clap of thunder hit the roof like a boulder.

'This is our chance, darling,' Lana shot into Marco's ear. 'The rain is so loud, he'll never hear us. Fuck me, hard.'

Lana sat on Marco, and began to rotate to his thrusts. She was urgent, her hands stretching for support to the low roof. Everything and everyone had gone crazy in the storm. She imagined other couples in every car and taxi copulating right across London. The whole traffic queue would be creaking on its suspension. Nymphomania and erotomania would be symptoms of the electric storm. They began to establish a rapid rhythm. She fitted her legs right over his shoulders, and he adapted her to his need. They'd abandoned all care that the taxi was rocking with their impassioned lovemaking.

Another violent feeler of lightning blazed a yellow trail across the sky. The rain increased, as their excitement mounted. They were conscious only of the storm and their mounting climax. Neither would be able to hold back much longer. The wave mounted simultaneously. Marco knew he couldn't delay, and Lana too, was straining towards violent orgasm. They twisted round a volcanic core, she arched back in an agonized scream, as he drove his hot come into her. They were both so ecstatic that they almost lost consciousness in the intensity of orgasm, and then they clung to each other in the aftermath, soothed by the drumming rain and the conspiratorial envelope it had placed over the city.

It seemed like they had been quiet a long time, before the taxi started up again in the diminishing rain. They could hear the storm going off like a big cat after the kill.

'What was the hotel you wanted, governor?' The cabbie growled through the partition, as though it was an ordinary London day, and the storm something inconsequential that would blow away into the blue.

Catching Stars

'Not so fast,' Sandra cautioned, as her lover made to enter her, fitting his body over hers with the sort of intermeshing fluency they had established over months of dynamic sex. 'You haven't heard my story yet, and if you don't interrupt me and just allow yourself to grow excited, then it will be even better.'

Nick rolled over on to his back, his taut erection periscoping for his navel, his willingness to wait being part of the arousal games they had devised to enhance pleasure. It had become a habit. Neither would allow the other orgasmic pleasure until they had exhausted the range of delayed excitation.

'If you don't lie back and listen, I shall have to put you in leather handcuffs again,' Sandra whispered, 'and you'll have to tie my feet in black ribbon to prevent me caressing your penis with my toes. I know how you like that. It takes ages to come, but it's worth it.'

Nick lay back and didn't protest. He knew that Sandra's story would be the prolegomena to some form of perverse sexual geometry. He reached for his champagne glass and listened to the fizz on his tongue. It reminded him of childhood, and how as a boy he had placed a shell to his ear and believed that the roar of his blood was the ocean laying white thunder across the beach. He was wearing a pair of elbow-length black silk gloves, for Sandra nurtured an adventurous fetish to have black silk fingers playing over her bottom.

'What I'm going to tell you is completely true,' Sandra added, momentarily slipping under the sheets to place a lipsticked kiss on Nick's cock. 'I was at a private girls' school between the ages of twelve and seventeen. There weren't any boys so we pretended to be them at times. We used to wear bottle-green gym-slips and pleated games skirts, and little white cotton panties underneath. In order to get out of conventional games like hockey, a number of us gained permission to experiment with juggling. I had silver juggling balls, but other friends used red, pink, green or blue. It used to look like we were negotiating miniature planets, sci-fi toys that had somehow dropped out of the sky into our hands. I used to juggle opposite Julie, who defied school convention by wearing black knickers under her games skirt. I used to catch glimpses of them each time she retrieved a dropped ball. I found myself paying scrupulous attention to what all the girls were wearing under their uniforms. We had already elected a place behind the bicycle shed where we taught each other french-kissing.

'I had adopted the role of an imaginary boy called James and, with my hair piled under a beret, the girl I was designated was no other than Julie. Of course this was innocent enough. We began by kissing lightly and then deepening the lips to an oval, and then I advanced my tongue. It went into her mouth like a pink fish and began swimming in her saliva. It felt like I was tasting a new form of fruit, soft and pulpy like melon. When Julie reciprocated the action, all the movie kisses we had watched seemed in the process of being consummated. And suddenly all the girls were doing it. There were eight of us paired off into four couples. It didn't go any further that day, but Julie gave us a wonderful demonstration of three-ball juggling, the metallic blue spheres perfectly co-ordinated in their reach and fall, and Julie occasionally kicking her legs high like a cancan dancer.'

Nick leaned over and placed a hot mouth on Sandra's left nipple. He switched to the right with equal effect, and watched her close her eyes in order to luxuriate in the sensation. Then taking out one of the lengths of black ribbon he kept concealed under the pillow, he slid down her body, flickering his tongue over her moist vulva, a crack swollen to the density of a purple pansy, and went all the way down her legs to her ankles.

'You're going to be punished for not telling enough,' Nick warned, and began binding her ankles together with ribbon. He tightened the knot, and confident it was secure, resurfaced for air. 'The next time,' he admonished, 'it will be your thighs and then your wrists. And you'll be begging to be fucked, and unable to get your legs open.'

Sandra moaned at the constriction of her ankles. She arched her legs and importuned, 'Lick me. Bury your head between my legs.'

Nick didn't respond. He lay there, coolly imperturbable. 'I want to hear how you licked Julie,' he replied. 'If it wasn't that day it was the next one.'

'I'll let you in a little on my secrets,' Sandra volunteered. 'Julie and I began flirting in class. But it was more than the usual schoolgirl thing. It was leading to something serious. Her green eyes would meet mine across the room and I'd catch my breath. And once when we sat next to each other in the French class she placed my hand on her lap. The thrill went through me like lightning. I could feel her warmth and her legs were trembling with excitement. And soon after that there was the occasion when we almost collided in the corridor. Knocked off balance I swung round and our lips became involved in a kiss that went to the roots of my sex. It was then that I knew it would happen. For days I lived in suspense. We seemed to avoid each other in preparation for the meeting when it happened. And meanwhile general activities near the bicycle sheds hadn't diminished. Girls would go there after school to play at being boys. And of course the roles were exchanged. Sometimes we were boys and sometimes girls. Both roles were exciting.'

'You'll have to be punished again, for not telling the true story,' said Nick, again slipping beneath the sheets and causing Sandra to giggle as he paid attention to her pussy with his tongue. 'Now I'm going to tie your thighs with ribbon,' he remonstrated, and Sandra made playful attempts to elude his designs before submitting to the second phase of her punishment. 'Now I want the real story,' Nick commanded.

'But I shouldn't be telling you these things,' said Sandra. 'You'll begin to think I really like having sex with girls. And perhaps I do. But I'll tell you the story of how Julie and I came together, providing that you release me.'

'Only if it's good enough,' Nick consented. 'If it isn't I'll have to tie your wrists as well.'

'It happened on a Friday morning. I still remember the day exactly. Julie wasn't at lessons that day, but her friend Marcella handed me a note. I remember taking it to the toilets and locking myself in a cubicle. And it was there in the conspiratorial quiet that I read Julie's love letter. She told me that she had stayed away from school today as she wanted to lie in bed and think of me. She asked if I would come to her house the next day, on the Saturday evening. She said that her parents were away on holiday in Greece. We would have the place to ourselves.'

'Quicker,' said Nick, 'or you'll have your wrists tied.'

'I spent all afternoon preparing for our rendezvous. I had a long bath, and after the fashion of a Japanese pornographic magazine which had been passed about at school, I depilated myself. I put on a bright red lipstick and a pair of my mother's little black panties which I filched from her drawer. I can remember it all to the last detail. I was so sensitive to touch that I would have jumped if a stranger had even imagined making love to me. I would have seen the idea in his head stand out like a red fish in a transparent bowl.'

'I want more details about your preparation,' said Nick. 'And remember, I may not stop at tying your wrists. There may be further indignities.'

'I wore skintight jeans and a skimpy black jumper, and a black bra which gave a conical shape to my breasts,' said Sandra. 'I knew precisely what I was entertaining. And when Julie opened the door she looked twenty and not sixteen. She was dressed in a black leather mini-skirt and sheer seamed tights. She kissed me full on the lips by way of greeting. And that exploratory kiss went so deep into me it was like a probe.

'Julie poured me a drink. We were neither of us used to alcohol, and the martini cocktail which Julie proportioned placed me somewhere else in my head. The alcohol induced lateral thinking. We were trying to discuss our first readings of Proust, but all the time Julie was sitting opposite me in an armchair with her legs arched, so that I could see right up her skirt. I can't remember at what point she came over and sat on my lap. It was unexpected, but it felt natural. We began kissing, and for the first time my hands wandered to her full breasts. Julie purred, and instructed me to place my hand under her jumper. When I did, she bit my neck from passion, and advised me how to caress her nipples. And I was conscious that she seemed much more sexually experienced than me, but I couldn't work out how she had acquired this knowledge. I think I told myself that she had probably read erotic novels, and knew from those the intimate vocabulary of sensuality. But I was frightened by her excitement.

'She began to push herself against me, and the breasts which I had extracted from her bra were suddenly being placed in my face. Their nipples were splashed purple. Julie said that the circular zone of each nipple was called the areola. I had areolas. And I was getting stimulated by her excitement. She had placed a hand between her legs while I was arousing her nipples, and now she slipped my hand to that accommodating role.'

'You're going to have to be tied completely,' said Nick, taking out a short length of black ribbon, and proceeding to lick Sandra's breasts as he went in search of her hidden hands. She was sitting on them, and attempted to keep them concealed, so that Nick had to turn her over and spank her round bottom to have her liberate her hands.

'Now I can do what I like with you,' he affirmed. 'I want to hear far more than you're telling me. And stay lying on your stomach, so that I can discipline you if necessary. Without hands or feet there's nothing you can do to retaliate.'

'I was telling you that Julie placed my hand on the wet divide between her legs. She pleaded with me to tickle her. She told me that the man always took the dominant mode of action. And I delighted in tickling her. She slipped out of her tights and skirt with alacrity, so as to give me easier access to her sex. By now I was really getting turned on and losing the inhibitions I may have brought to the game. And what's more, the action I was imparting to her seemed to be transmitted to myself. In tickling her I was tickling myself. That's the good thing about gay sex, you know precisely how the other person feels because you've also been there. There isn't any of that wondering how the opposite receives pleasure.

'And the next thing was that my jeans were being pulled off, and not without effort as they were very tight. Julie said she was going to do something to me that she wished me to copy, and that it would feel incredible. She began kissing my navel and then working her lips lower. I sort of knew what was coming, but couldn't imagine the feeling. Suddenly her lips were hot on my panties, her fingers lifting an elasticated ridge so her tongue could work in underneath. And once I let go and placed my legs over her shoulders, the sensation was incredible. I couldn't have imagined it was this good. I found myself relaxed enough to build towards climax. I was shouting for more and more, while she rimmed me with an alacritous tongue.'

'And what did you give her?' Nick commanded, rewarding Sandra for her narrative by running a line of kisses down her spine to the crack of her bottom. He lingered there with his tongue, then worked his way back on the same sensitive route to her nape. She shivered convulsively and bit her lips.

'I gave her the same. She must have performed oral sex on me for an hour, and then she told me to come upstairs. I went with her to the bedroom, most of my clothes leaving a trail behind me on the living room carpet. And once upstairs she positioned her legs in the way she had positioned mine, and I began to savour her pussy. It was hot and saline and very urgent.

I teased it with the tip of my tongue, watching the little bud expand. Julie urged me to put my tongue right in, and later on my fingers. She wanted to feel all of me. Julie began reaching orgasm after orgasm, her clit was so sensitive. We both looked like we had been sitting in a sauna for the evening. We were both so concentrated on pleasure that I didn't hear the bedroom door open.'

'Get on with the story and you'll be properly rewarded,' said Nick. 'But remember, one digression, and you'll be additionally bound.'

'I was working away at Julie's clit when I felt a tongue flick across my pussy from behind. I was up on all fours, and the sensation darted like moist fire between my legs. There wasn't any chance to scream, for Julie came forward and sealed my mouth in a long kiss. I couldn't speak, and all the time this tongue was continuing to take liberties with my sex.

'I was now being held firmly from behind, and Julie hissed in my ear, "Don't look round, but it's my brother. I thought I would introduce a real man into the game." My initial feelings of revulsion were disappearing. I could feel his enflamed member brushing against my bottom. It felt like an addition to his body, as though something indomitably hard was struggling to break into me.'

'I suppose it slipped up your crack from the rear, or up your arse?' prompted Nick.

'You forget, I was a virgin,' said Sandra. 'It's not that easy to deflower someone. Anyhow, I enjoyed the sensation of being kissed by two people, one from the front and one behind.'

'You're not telling the truth,' warned Nick. 'One more slip and you'll be bound a second time round the thighs.' That said, he went down on her again and tentatively aroused her with his tongue. She pleaded with him to continue, but he came up again for air, and checked that the knots binding her wrists were secure. Under no circumstances would he risk her touching herself at the volcanic core. When he entered her he wanted her to explode.

'I'll tell you more about the game,' Sandra said, 'but carry on licking me.'

Nick refused, despite the fact that his orgasm was tingling as a subtext in his scrotum. 'Tell me the truth,' he demanded.

'I am,' said Sandra. 'I hadn't even turned round to see this brother of Julie's. All I could feel was his tongue and his cock drumming against me. It was huge, like yours, and I could feel that it was moist at the tip. Eventually I disengaged myself from their caresses, and fought free of the boy's urgency. He was made up to look like a girl, something that evidently excited him. His lips were a smudged strawberry lipstick, and the inexpert application of eyeliner gave him two black eyes. His face was white with foundation. Julie informed me that he wanted me to put on my dark green games skirt and white cotton panties and blow him.

'I went even further. I dressed in Julie's mother's stockings and suspenders and sat in front of him nibbling an apple with my legs wide open. We decided to take it in turn. Julie began by licking her brother's cock, and I was the support act. You know it's not uncommon for brothers and sisters at that age to play with each other. It's only a game. He began to grow visibly more excited, and I took over. At that age I'd never sucked cock. I was surprised how big it was in my mouth. And in order to make him wait I'd leave off for a few seconds, take a bite from my red apple and resume sucking in a disinterested manner. We were so precocious, and he loved it. Julie left me to it, and went and sat on the sofa and tickled herself in her black knickers, to add to her brother's excitement. He was moaning now, and the whole length began to twitch. I could hardly contain his thrusts, and then his come began to decant in hot spurts. It went on and on. It was like catching stars. White-hot shooting stars in my mouth. Star after star after star. And if he fucked me later, I'm not going to tell until you do.'

'I have to untie some of the ribbons first,' said Nick, and he began with the ankles and the thighs and then the waist. He would leave her hands tied. And when he entered her it was with explosive urgency. And she, as his urgency increased, tickled his balls with a single finger, the one on which she wore a ring decorated with stars.

Tainted Love

Johnny kept on scanning the scrap of pink paper a French girl had given him on the tube ride between Regent's Park and Piccadilly Circus. It contained a name, Brigitte, a telephone number, and a prominent red heart with a dagger piercing it, the latter drawn hastily, but clearly identifiable.

The whole thing had come as a surprise. Johnny had got on at Regent's Park, and had found himself seated opposite a foreign girl whose big green eyes appeared instantly attracted to him, as though she had been waiting all her life for this particular moment, and had singled Johnny out to be the recipient of her favours. Johnny recollected her blond hair, done up à la young Bardot, her green drop-earrings, and the extraordinarily short skirt she was wearing, a micro that disappeared to her hips like a strip of black belt. Her long, fish-net legs were draped one over the other. Johnny had succumbed totally to her spell, and their eyes had worked at each other like the mixing of two paints. Johnny had watched the girl hastily extract a notebook and pen from her handbag, and hurriedly write down the details he now reviewed at home. She had decamped a stop before him, pressing the note into his hand, and he had gasped at the sight of her legs beginning to disappear up the Exit stairs.

Hours later, as he sat on his bed, his erection triggering at the prospect of realizing his sexual fantasies through Brigitte, Johnny prepared himself to make a call. He was already imagining Brigitte in the yogic plough position, her legs folded right over her head with her feet on the floor, a posture that would give his tongue delicious access to her twat. Facing the other way, and kneeling, it would look like he was drinking from a fountain between her legs.

It was all too good. Brigitte teased her w's for r's into a seductive vocabulary, additionally surprising Johnny by telling him with a change of tone that she hoped he would give her 'tainted love'. This was no linguistic slip, and Johnny found himself cracking his zip open while they continued to speak, his cock rasping for attention. They arranged to meet at eight o'clock the following night outside Green Park station, as Brigitte explained she was temporarily living in a flat in Half Moon Street. She blew him a kiss down the phone, and the line went dead, the big spaces of the capital closing over them like surf.

Johnny pondered the extraordinary circumstances governing their proposed rendezvous. Brigitte hadn't even asked for his surname, address, or telephone number, but that sucked if she was simply looking for a transient fling. Johnny got to thinking of her fish-net thighs again, and too excited to go without, worked himself off to a riotously orgiastic climax.

All the next day he waited for night. There was an orchestrated excitement in his solar plexus, and he found it difficult to concentrate on the video he was editing for television release. His mind kept on going back to Brigitte, and fast-forwarding to the imagined prospects of sex that night. Would she tongue his cock to a seasoned pâté? Would he stick it in the spaces between her toes? His testosterone level was simmering, and erections kept on intruding on his work. In the way that an opera singer can break a glass with the directed power of her voice, so he wanted Brigitte's throaty orgasm to smash a window with the intensity of its ecstatic gutturals. And he wanted his come to mix with her lipstick, like the colour of strawberry ice-cream.

Johnny listened to the sampling on the video soundtrack, and decided to go home. He walked across the park, his eyes burning into the bottom of a girl wearing skintight jeans. He kept those round, compact proportions in his focus for as long as he could, curves enhanced by the girl wearing high heels. When he got home he showered, called a number of friends, put on an Aretha Franklin CD, and relaxed. He still had two hours to pass before the time of his intended meeting with Brigitte at Green Park.

He pondered on the definition of tainted love. There was the song of that name, a Northern soul number; originally sung by Gloria Jones, the song had achieved international success through Soft Cell, a duo whose infamous reputation for sleaze and backroom bars had invited media sensationalism. The singer with Soft Cell, Marc Almond, had come to stand for a black eye-linered imp, a man whose private life was the speculative fancy of every tabloid.

That was one definition of tainted love. But Johnny reflected on how the lyrics were comparatively harmless, and were only afforded a double meaning by Almond's adopted bondage gear, and sexually ambiguous image. Like those of most pop songs, the lyrics were essentially about unrequited love. There was the sort of tainted love attributed to Oscar Wilde, but Brigitte couldn't mean this. But whatever, there was a distinct flavour of decadence to her proposal, and Johnny let his imagination run riot with the subject. Tainted meant corrupted, contaminated, stained, blemished – not the sort of associations he would have afforded a glamorous young French girl. But why had she picked on him? His mind kept returning to that question. Brigitte's looks were exceptional, and while Johnny was reasonably good-looking, he wasn't that distinguished.

As he splashed a little Chanel cologne on his torso, it suddenly jumped out at him. In the old days, and in imitation of Marc Almond, he had had a Gutterhearts tattoo worked on his lower right arm. Yesterday, he had been wearing a white cotton shirt with the sleeves rolled up, and Brigitte must have recognized the red and blue tattoo, with a dagger piercing a flaming heart, standing out on his arm. It was a sign to a complicitous cult. Johnny satisfied himself that this would account for Brigitte's reference to tainted love, but he was still marginally disquieted, and it was this tension which contributed to his sexual excitement.

Johnny paid special attention to his appearance. He put on a white cotton shirt and black trousers, and snaked a red belt through the loops. He gelled his hair back in a Presley quiff, and slipped on a pair of patent leather ankle-boots. He looked good, and the little diamond stud in his ear glinted like a star. He would conquer Brigitte and be tainted in the process.

The minutes were dragging by. He played music and consulted his watch, and tried to banish sexual fantasies from his mind. He was already overexcited, and hoped the tube wouldn't be full of girls in mini-skirts, the foreign tourists who swarmed into London exuding hot blood and sexuality.

When Johnny got on the tube his worst expectations were realized. He found himself in a compartment full of mini-skirted tourists, and his eye registered a strip of black gusset, as a blond thing rearranged her tanned legs under a floaty wisp of a skirt. It was all too much, black gussets, white gussets, and Johnny felt the bulge in his crotch tightening.

He was glad to decamp from the sexual heat of the compartment, and he hurried into the milling entrance of the station foyer. There was Brigitte, dressed as she had been on the previous day, with men's eyes running over her body like a swarm of glinting flies. It amused Johnny to think of men dispersing into all different parts of the city, with Brigitte's image exciting their respective fantasies. Wankers would be manoeuvring her into positions all night.

Brigitte was compliant to Johnny's demonstrative greeting, and he found himself kissing her directly on the lips. Her response was immediate and feverish. Her kiss tasted of summer in the South. 'Let's walk in Greek Park a bit,' she suggested, and as naturally as if they had been a couple for years, Johnny fitted his arm around Brigitte's waist, and felt the rhythmic undulation of her hips as she walked. It was still light, although the dark was coming on, and couples were dotted under the trees, or sat on benches. They entered directly into easy conversation, and talked of their mutual longing to be by the blue sea, and of little things – families, backgrounds, the moment, the alienation that large cities bring to the individual. And still Johnny didn't raise the subject of how or why they had met, and all the improbabilities surrounding that meeting. He was completely under Brigitte's spell; the seductive qualities of her voice, her natural vivacity, her curvaceous body, her whole mysterious ambience left him fascinated. It was like time had suddenly stopped as they crossed the park, and chose a towering chestnut tree under which to sit, as the night advanced.

Despite her absolutely minimal skirt Brigitte sat down beside Johnny, their shoulders touching, their togetherness fluent, and their first kiss followed almost immediately. Their lips hungrily found each other, and formed a sustained circular motion. Brigitte's tongue slid into the back of Johnny's throat, and his hands correspondingly traced the outline of her prominent nipples poking through her red top. She was braless, and her breasts were conically plump like avocados. Johnny kneaded her nipples, and drew from her excited gasps, his tongue exploring her neck, and hers complementing his discovery of sensitive nerves, and soon he was lying fully on top of Brigitte, his erection beating out a drum rhythm on her pubic areas, and her skirt disappearing to her navel as they fitted their bodies together in a preliminary try-out for the sex which they knew would come later. It was all too perfect, and a nagging sense of disquiet continued to occupy Johnny's mind. He glued himself to Brigitte's body, and in his urgency contemplated entering her there on the grass, under the heavy shadow of the chestnut tree – only that seemed to make something too easy of the situation. There was much more excitement to come, and Johnny preferred to hold back, despite the encouragement of Brigitte's caresses.

Her fingers were already travelling the sensitive highway between his balls and the tip of his cock, a route that she electrified with her fingertips. Johnny felt a volcanic rage in his groin, a glow that suffused every point in his body. They lay together, unwilling to separate, their bodies lighting each other up, and gently, without causing any disequilibrium, Brigitte pointed out the coolness in the night air, and she suggested they go back to her place in Half Moon Street.

It was barely a ten-minute walk, and on the way there Brigitte explained that she was in London to improve her English, and was working as a home-help to a family who allowed her her own little apartment in their town house. They were away for a few days, and Brigitte was using the leisure time to see the sights in London. Johnny noted how men in the streets danced their eyes over Brigitte's assets, and her body rippled to each affirmative pressure his hand applied to her waist. They walked back leisurely, drinking in the night air, and both dazzled by the ease they expressed in each other's company. And again Johnny wavered on the brink of asking Brigitte why she had acted so impulsively in handing him that note on the tube, and again he failed to take the initiative.

Brigitte's apartment was upstairs, and Johnny followed her as she climbed the stairs, his eyes taking in nothing but the limitless expanse of fish-net thighs. He was both apprehensive and excited, and a fraction afraid he might be sprung inside her flat. For a moment he thought of retreating, bolting back to the street, and forgoing the prospect of pleasure which awaited him.

But it was too late, and Brigitte opened the door to a tasteful, dimly lit apartment, the shaded green lamps throwing light over a sumptuous sofa and chairs, the whole place appearing elegant, modern, and well furnished. Brigitte collapsed into a chair, and simultaneously reached over for the sound system. Johnny listened as the familiar synth bars of 'Tainted Love' sounded in the room, and the even more familiar Almond vocals took up the theme. The voice, singing theatrically flat, told the story of a ruinously perverse love, and brought back all manner of associations to Johnny, the summer in which he had first heard the song, and the girls he had met on holiday that year. For a time he had become a Soft Cell aficionado, and so his eventual gravitation to the iconic Gutterhearts tattoo.

Johnny sat in the chair closest to Brigitte, and at first it appeared as though the spell had broken, and that they had suddenly grown cold, awkward in finding speech, and set apart by their being total strangers to each other. Even Johnny's sexual alertness had vanished. The song was part of a compilation CD, and Johnny found himself relistening to other Soft Cell favourites like 'Memorabilia' and 'Say Hello Wave Goodbye'.

Brigitte shifted in her chair, taking up various seductive poses, and then right out of the blue, she said, 'Johnny, it was your tattoo I noticed first; I saw in you a conspirator. I wanted to know you, and see if we could have a little tainted love. I too have a tattoo, a heart and dagger, but you can't see it. You'll have to discover its existence.'

Brigitte came over to Johnny's chair, and sat on his lap, and placed her arms around his neck. His desire returned instantaneously, and he slipped his hand into the soft divide between her legs and coaxed that moist little valley. Brigitte responded with passionate rollings of her bottom over Johnny's now indomitable erection. She turned round to face him, scissoring her legs around his back, and working her crotch on to his pointed bulge. Johnny rolled her fish-net tights back, a movement she assisted all the way to her ankles and down over them, her scarlet panties jumping into view. He was so urgent he wanted to shred her panties with his teeth, and his tongue snaked into the wet divide of her crack. He picked her up and carried her to the deep sofa. Brigitte playfully wriggled, scratched, tickled, and kicked her legs into the air, and ended up facing the opposite way to Johnny, her lips swallowing on his cock, while his tongue eagerly enquired of her pussy.

Johnny could hardly hold back. Her deep throating rhythm tongued him to ecstasy, and was so relentless in its movements, that he let go and chased a hot jet of come into her throat. He was still excited, and remained erect, while Brigitte sucked the remaining drops from his cock, and once again teased his length from the base to the tip.

Johnny snapped off Brigitte's scarlet panties, tearing them

from her bottom, and there the tattoo was on her right buttock cheek, but low down, and the words 'Tainted Love' were written on the red heart. Johnny placed his mouth to the spot, and placed a love bite on the surrounding area.

'There's another one too, in the front,' said Brigitte, and Johnny manoeuvred her on to her back and saw the tiny tattoo on her shaved triangle. Johnny couldn't hold back any longer, he plunged into Brigitte, and a shriek escaped from her lips. He rode her furiously, and her voice orchestrated the pleasure she was receiving. And when she came – her nails sunk into his back, her body synchronized to his every thrust – it was with an agonized scream. They lay together, his tattooed arm draped around her tattooed bottom, and brought together by 'Tainted Love'.

He Was a She

Martin sat in a gold swivel-chair five storeys up above Chelsea Harbour, reviewing the river's glaucous spine, and watching a tourist ferry negotiate a grey-green passage through the toxic undertow of the city's effluvia. It was an afternoon in late July, and a haze sat over the precinct like a thumbprint indented on a photograph. He could just make out the figures of three Japanese girls walking round the harbour beneath him, all of them dressed in tight, washed-out jeans. One of them had dyed her hair a dramatic scarlet, and he imagined its silky texture resembling a poppy's fragility.

Martin worked as a literary agent. His mind was fogging out from a surfeit of undistinguished fiction. Most of it was too full-frontal and lacked imaginative space. The writing was too close to what it described, and so there was no dimension on which the imagination could operate. Martin disliked the flat surfaces of social realism in the same way as he felt an antipathy to men who identified only with their masculine role. He liked the harmony established by dualities, the imagination in prose as it transformed the external world into a tangent of surprise, and the dichotomy in men who released the feminine within them by living out the fantasy of being transvestites.

Martin wondered how his colleagues would react if they knew that beneath his sober black trousers he was wearing a black suspender belt, pink silk panties and fish-net stockings. His fetishistic obsession with female lingerie had begun early, and had been linked to the intense but unfulfilled sexual desire he had felt for his sister, Janine. Catching glimpses of her in her bra and panties, watching her button her lips with scarlet lipstick or meticulously delineate her eyes with a black eyeliner pencil, had engendered in him a corresponding propensity to emulate her pronounced femininity. And when she was out, and he found himself alone and moody in the house on a Sunday afternoon, the silence punctuated only by Bessie Smith's brokenhearted blues, then he would begin the ritual of trying on Janine's flimsy black panties, and making up his lips and eyes with innovative flourishes that came instinctively rather than by studied emulation. Dressing up had caused him to realize extreme excitement, so too the thrill contained in the danger that he might be discovered. All he knew was that the need was ungovernable, and the risk negligible compared to the stimulus of the act.

Over the years cross-dressing had grown to be something inseparable from his notion of sexual pleasure. Martin could find no anomaly in transvestism, and rather than its alienating him from women, he had discovered to the contrary that most sexually adventurous women found men in women's lingerie a big turn-on. But to Martin the chief pleasure lay in the element of surprise. He liked a woman's fingers to discover for the first time that he was wearing frilly transparent panties. Reactions varied considerably from deepening a woman's caress to having her withdraw her advances until he had reassured her of the provocativeness of his particular fetish. Either response afforded him pleasure, and he had grown to choose exclusive lingerie and to wear the sheerest Dior silk stockings.

Another ten minutes and Martin would be free to leave for the afternoon. He had taken to coming in early on the ferry and to leaving by mid-afternoon. In an hour's time he would meet Simone, a rendezvous he hoped would result in his taking her back to his apartment. He rejected the novel he was reading, the chunky wooden prose doing nothing to elevate its subject from routine platitude. He looked out over the harbour. The monochrome grey cloud was giving way to a blue sky ceiling.

Light was hitting off the river. Everything seemed transformed, as though he had stepped out of a cinema into reality. He read the sunlight as a propitious sign for his meeting with Simone.

Before he stepped into the lift to leave the building Martin went to the men's room. It fired him to think that he would check the seams of his stockings and apply perfume in a room visited by his apparently conventional colleagues. He had always derived kicks from violating gender restrictions. And often he had felt like flaunting his difference right in front of their eyes, and slipping back to his office in a red cocktail skirt. But he contented himself with locking a cubicle door and adjusting his seams in the inviolable silence of that unit. Wearing silk panties kept him permanently sensual and erect, and he looked on his chosen items of lingerie as a form of infallible aphrodisiac. He was hard and throbbing. He could feel the excitement chasing through his nerves, and he liked to think that he had found in Simone a woman who would respond with hot passion to his particular needs.

As he came out of the cubicle, and was checking his hair in front of the mirror, Paul breezed into the men's room. He was the youngest partner in the company, and Martin had noticed an almost imperceptible femininity in his face and manners which the young man worked hard to repress. It wasn't anything obvious, and probably nobody but Martin would have noticed. As Martin was leaving the room – he couldn't be sure – he thought he heard Paul remark, 'I know your habits, and I do it too!'

Martin walked to the lift, the phrase still ringing in his head, but he couldn't be sure if it had really been spoken by Paul, and he had no intention of going back to ask. The voice haunted him, but once out of the building and under a sheer blue sky curved above Cheyne Walk, he forgot the voice and excitedly anticipated his meeting with Simone.

He had purposely arranged to meet her in a wine bar close to his apartment, so that the transition from one to the other could be affected with ease. The place was dark, and Simone was sitting waiting for him, her leggy pose winning his immediate attention, her black micro-mini appearing as an incidental to her sheer black tights. She had on a stylish purple beret with matching lipstick. Already he was imagining her lips working that purple texture into his telescoping cock. She looked like a girl who would swallow all of it.

Martin liked to talk to women about scent, make-up, what was being worn on the catwalks, and he so avoided any discussion of literature that it was often with surprise that his female partner discovered that he worked as a literary agent.

This evening he felt inordinately aroused. On the previous occasion he had met with Simone his fingers had discovered the wetness between her thighs, and he had drawn from her the sinuous contortions of a body he now intended to convulse with orgasm. Her hands on that occasion had failed to discover his secret by going inside his fly, and had instead coaxed the outline of his cock through his tight-fitting jeans. If she had detected the presence of suspender straps through the skin-moulded denim, then she hadn't let on.

They sat and drank wine and talked, and Martin quickly began stroking Simone's legs, working his hands in long brush strokes from her knees to the tops of her thighs. He could feel his cock straining above the ridge of the little pink panties attempting to contain it. He was all the more excited to note, from the one time that she had rearranged her legs, that she too was wearing pink panties. It crossed his mind that they might even have purchased identical garments, something which would make their coming together a bizarre union of corresponding tastes. Simone was growing visibly excited, and from the deep protracted kisses she had started to give him, her tongue working in every corner of his mouth, he knew that the time would soon be right for him to suggest that they returned to his apartment.

Back home, he had everything prepared. The dark green blinds were snapped shut on the early summer evening, and subdued wall lighting gave the living-room just the right atmosphere for seduction. Martin had arranged vases of blue cornflowers and blue delphiniums on the glass tabletop, and Simone collapsed into the deep black sofa, her skirt riding to her waist as she attempted to bring it back to a level of decorum. Martin didn't miss the opportunity. He followed her on to the sofa, his body tumbling across hers in a series of erotic planes, his hands and lips going everywhere that tickled and drew excited laughter from her ecstatically thrown-back head.

And as her skirt went missing, so he could see through her ultra-sheer tights that she was wearing the same pink silk panties as the ones which were deliciously irritating his triggering cock. It was she who slipped out of her tights and skirt, and began dabbing scorching kisses across his nipples and navel. He tensed with the expectation of her discovery, and her tapered red fingernails began unzipping him with agonized suspense. She ran one finger, then two inside his fly, and he could tell by the injection of passion into her kiss and sensitized fingers that she was aroused by her discovery.

She opened the waistband of his trousers, and with his eyes closed he felt her lips run across his black suspender belt, while her fingers snapped the black straps against his thighs, just like a man does with a woman. Martin couldn't imagine sex that didn't involve this reversal of roles, and Simone was hungry to accommodate his needs. Her lips were brushing the head of his penis, and then with all the sensitive expertise of someone familiar with the gesture, she unclipped first one stocking and then the other and rolled them down Martin's legs until they bunched like two black flowers at his ankles. Simone was treating him with the tender sensuality of a man making love to a woman who demanded gentleness. She kissed his painted toenails through his stockings, and let her tongue travel up his thighs all the way to his scrotum, as though she were a man positioning herself for cunnilingus. Now he felt her tongue on his balls, and then she went back down his legs and began massaging his feet and finding nerve-points in his soles which connected directly with his cock.

'Let me make you up, before we go into the bedroom,' Simone whispered, and he abandoned himself to her precise artistry as she worked at his eyes with mascara, eye shadow and eyeliner, and then highlighted his cheeks with a dusting brush, before paying detailed attention to his lips, outlining them not only with lipstick but with a supporting gloss and a dark lip crayon. She was deeply concentrated on her task, and periodically she would draw her head back to examine the line of her art. Martin grew additionally excited by this pronounced attention to his looks, and delighted in the idea that he would have a woman's face and a man's rampant penis.

'Go and look in the mirror,' Simone advised, and Martin got up from the sofa and confronted an image in the mirror that he had always imagined to be himself, but had never thought to realize. This was the true him, the concealed feminine who lived on the inside awaiting release. And for the first time he felt truly at one with himself.

'You look unbelievably sexy,' Simone laughed, 'just edible –' and having said that she adopted a Spanish wiggle and led him into the bedroom.

Martin got Simone into the 69 position, and ran his tongue over her until she was juicy like a newly sliced melon. She had a shaved pubis, so he could bury his tongue in the folds of her labia. He was holding back his orgasm despite the depth to which Simone was swallowing him. The suction of her tongue was beginning to pressurize him towards explosion, and realizing this she backed off and urged him to slip into her pussy from behind. It was like all the fantasies he had ever nurtured gathered in the core of his sexual energy at that moment. He buried himself in her, and stayed dead still, letting her experience his hardness as a pivot, and she cried out with anticipation for his rooted thrusting. But instead, he increased her pleasure by having her wait. He whispered suggestions into her ear as he covered it with his lips, he ran a finger deep into the crack of her bottom. She was imprisoned on his hard lust, and he rotated her gently from the hips to give her a foretaste of the spasmic urgency that would follow.

Simone arched her head back to kiss him, and little by little he began to move inside her. She was still living with the expectation that he was going to withhold pleasure, and then he began to open up, and he ran his hands down to her hips and positioned them there in order to have her synchronize with his powerful spiral movements. Her orgasm was released in a series of agonized screams, her mouth twisted open in a rictus, her head collapsing on the bed as he fired hot stars into her interior.

They lay there too drained to speak, listening to the subdued hum of London traffic outside, and to the noise of people pouring through the evening streets.

'We'll make each other up again later,' Simone suggested in a feline post-orgasm voice, and Martin lay interlaced by her legs and arms, his desire beginning to find force again.

'You know what,' Simone confided, 'I went to bed with a young man called Paul, who also liked to dress up. He's also a literary agent. He's more conventional than you, but he was dressed similarly, only he got pleasure out of wearing panties and stockings under a grey pinstripe suit. The suit had to be grey, he told me.'

'What did he look like?' Martin enquired, trying to keep his voice impartial in its curiosity.

'He was blond, about thirty, considerate manners. Said his offices were in Chelsea. I dated him for a couple of weeks and the one time we went to bed, he was dressed rather like you. Pink panties, stockings and suspenders. He wanted me to make him up, and he asked me if he could keep my panties to wear at the office. I imagine he's doing just that. He was lonely, but he said there was someone at the office, a man with your name, Martin, who would sympathize. He told me he knew this person cross-dressed as he had once glimpsed an area of fish-net stocking showing on the man's calf when he had inadvertently scratched his ankle.'

'How very strange to think that there's another Martin who

also has my predisposition to cross-dress,' he found himself saying, as he took Simone's left nipple from his lips.

'But it's definitely not you,' Simone volunteered. 'You don't fit Paul's sketchy description of his colleague. He said this Martin sometimes wore lipstick at the office, and was an exhibitionist. You aren't. Besides, this man was older.'

Martin listened with curiosity to how his colleague perceived him, and felt confirmed in his belief that we invariably create a fiction for ourselves in describing another. But now he knew. Paul was walking around the office in a pair of Simone's flimsy panties. The thought excited him, and he decided that he too would win Simone's knickers, and have the secret satisfaction of having won even with Paul.

'I'd like to have your panties,' Martin ventured to Simone.

'You'll have to win them,' she teased. 'I will give them to you as a trophy, if you make me come again, like you did a short time ago.'

'Let me make you up this time,' Martin begged, and he applied to Simone's face the care and attention she had given to his. A little touching up from her, and their looks were almost identical. He lacquered her toes with the same scarlet nail polish he used on his own, fitted her legs round his waist and entered her to the hilt. From the very first thrust and her corresponding cry, he knew he was going to win his desired trophy.

He couldn't help smiling to himself to think that two men on the fifth floor of an office tower above Chelsea Harbour would both be wearing Simone's panties beneath their formal office clothes.

Hunt the Sequin

She sat on the bed, legs arched, fastidiously applying a coat of Russian-red nail varnish to her toes. She liked the sensual pleasure she derived from this intimate artistry, an expression that was both sexual and aesthetic. Her boyfriend was, more than any other man she had known, unfailingly appreciative of this detail. In fact, he would often insist on applying the lacquer to her toenails, and the sensations induced by him stroking the soles of her feet in the process of his painting her nails red, violet, green or black, would often lead to her experiencing orgasm. And at times she would reciprocate the ritual, and paint his toenails colours that corresponded to her own. He too, if she tickled his feet for long enough, would reach an orgasm. It was one of their private games, and had developed into a shared fetish.

Lavinia wanted to make it as a singer. She had the necessary voice and looks. Her black hair poured in snaking ringlets to her shoulders, her high cheekbones and triangular mouth were offset by green eyes, and her figure looked body-sprayed into a black top and skintight jeans. She'd set up a small home recording unit, and sang torch songs of the kind that divas like Judy Garland, Juliette Greco, Dusty Springfield, and Marc Almond gave to the world: tear-jerking, lonelier than blue ballads which went straight to the solitary places in the heart. And even at home, when practising with no audience but her own projected persona, she would wear a dress made of thousands of shocking-pink sequins. Moulded to the chiffon on which the sequins were sewn, she would balance on bruised suede stilettos, her mouth smudged the colour of crushed raspberry, and a wineglass placed within easy reach. Lavinia was adept at staging her own performances. She longed to take her talents a step further and acquire a live audience.

She saw herself as a sob sister, committed to her belief in unrequited love and the self-sacrifice that love demands. Her wounded, tremulous themes looked back to French chanson, as well as to the more jazz-influenced blues sung by the likes of Billie Holiday and Dinah Washington. She had begun to accumulate the accoutrements of a torch singer: a variety of boas, and elbow-length gloves in black satin, decorated her make-up table. She found she could use her voice in an operatic vibrato style, although she tempered this with a less elevated delivery, and was intent on developing a style of singing that was popular rather than histrionic.

Her boyfriend had warned her of the dissolute end that had come to most of the women who had pursued singing as a career, but she would only dismiss the decadent myth surrounding femmes fatales. Lavinia felt she had to honour her particular calling. Some minor interest had been expressed in her demo tapes, although the scout had suggested that she sing lyrics which were less emotionally charged.

One day her boyfriend came back to find her hunting sequins. A fall of these had occurred when she had unzipped her dress, and he found her arched on the floor, bottom up, desperate to retrieve the sequins she would sew back on her dress. 'Help me, darling,' she cried, as he extended a forefinger and tickled her in a arc that ran from her pussy to the crack of her bottom. 'Find my lost sequins, and you can demand what you want,' she said, shivering at the sensitivity with which he tickled her between the legs.

Steve joined in the search, using his eyes like pins to pick up the shimmering pink discs. 'You can't imagine what this dress means to me,' she continued. 'It's part of my true identity. I couldn't sing without it, and I've got my first gig coming up next week, an opening spot at the Fetish Club.'

'You'll be brilliant,' Steve said, hunting along the strip where a green carpet skirted the wooden floorboards. He dabbed at the offending glitterbugs, holding up two on the point of a finger as though he had been jabbed with a pin, and had produced a coagulative spot of shocking-pink blood.

The sight of Lavinia's bottom was causing him to lose concentration. He continued his absurd exploration of crevices in the boards, and of dab-the-spot on the carpet.

'We're getting there,' Lavinia exclaimed. 'And you'll be rewarded for your achievements.' He again slipped a finger between her wet lips as she went up on her haunches. And a little more incisively, and as a pointer to what would come, he sunk his teeth playfully into her left buttock.

'Not yet,' she laughed, 'I can still see more sequins on the carpet. I'll be your captive only when you've completed the task.'

'Make me yours, while we continue the search,' he said. 'I want you to make it impossible for me to unzip my jeans, but at the same time I need to be flexible so I can assist with the hunt. Handcuffs won't do, and nor will tying my wrists with a scarf or a pair of your panties.'

Again he excited her, this time by extending his tongue, and leaving a silver snail-trail across her crocth. She was so moist it was like she had been dreaming of a waterfall of orgasmic juices pouring through her body, and had woken to connect with the reality of the situation. Her pussy made a drinking sound each time he touched it.

Steve could feel his erection establishing a drum-beat against his stomach.

'I know a way to keep you in,' Lavinia said mischievously. 'But it will have to be handcuffs, and you'll collect the sequins with the tip of your tongue.'

Having said this, she went into the bedroom and reappeared with a pair of soft blue leather handcuffs. Having secured Steve's wrists, she returned to an even more provocative pose, bottom up, her hands working across her buttocks, with one finger straying to her pussy. Handcuffed, he could only protrude his tongue, like a cat in the sun, and imagine the tangy flavour of the juices flowing liberally from her cunt. They contained something of the smell of dank ivy leaves on a castle wall, and cinnamon as it lightly spices the palate. And whenever he licked Lavinia, with the slow flourish of a painter working on a particular detail of the canvas, she would moan with a convulsive shudder. It was her display of guttural vocalism that excited him to stage one audacity after the other, each being received with an increased response to pleasure.

'I hope you're picking up sequins with your tongue,' she laughed, returning to her own close scrutiny of the carpet. 'I'd never find sequins to match these; I got the dress at a charity shop, and it was undoubtedly made for a stage artist.'

Wanting to play the game, Steve crawled across his area of carpet, inspecting it for pink sequins, and retrieving a cluster with the tip of his tongue. He moved over to the low round table that occupied a central position in the room, and there Lavinia took the sequins off his tongue. It was tedious work, but to reward her captive Lavinia began to give open displays of masturbation. She sat facing him, legs wide open, and with two scarlet fingernails, proceeded to caress her pussy. She then rolled over in a half-somersault position, and pushing her black gusset aside, began to dip her fingers into her sensitive nerve-endings.

'If only your hands were free,' she taunted Steve, 'you could be giving me such pleasure. I like it when you roll my clitoris between your thumb and forefinger. I'm going to paint your nails, bad boy, while you're handcuffed, and then have you tickle me when you're released.' Lavinia continued to simulate sex positions, and then returned to assiduously combing the carpet for missing discs to her dress.

'We'll soon be there,' she said after a time. 'And now I'm going to unzip you so I can see what you've got.' Lavinia went over and slipped her tongue into Steve's mouth like a drinking straw inserted into a cocktail. At the same time, and with exaggerated slowness, she inched the zipper down over his engorged length. It had the mauve blush of an orchid, the tip straining out of the elastic of his tight black briefs. 'One little lick, and no more,' she said, fitting an oval mouth softly over the circumcised helmet. Steve gasped, and to complete her expertise, Lavinia took his length right into her mouth, squeezed it with pressure, and left him to anticipate the rhythmic head he knew would eventually follow.

'There's still more sequins to find, darling,' she teased. 'I can see them signalling for rescue.'

They resumed their diligent search; it was growing to be obsessive, and Lavinia had taken to walking round the room swinging her hips like a strip artist. If Steve had been able to place his hands round her bottom at such times he would have had the impression that he was steering a car round the wide sweep of a mountain bend.

'We're not through yet,' Lavinia warned in her playful tone. 'Focus carefully, I want the last shimmering offenders.'

'What is my reward going to be?' Steve questioned, propelling himself across the carpet on his knees, and shaking his manacled hands.

'It's up to you to ask,' Lavinia answered. 'Who knows how far I'll go to please you? My throat is being trained to deliver arias and coloratura. I'm sure it needs the silent pitch that comes with fellatio.'

'I'm not sure I'll settle for so little,' Steve replied, jabbing at a solitary pink sequin with his flickering tongue. 'I'm beginning to feel like an anteater, or a bird pecking for seeds, and my cock is boiling with hot lava.'

Lavinia went over to the microphone stand, draped the pink-sequinned dress across her front, put on a backing tape, and delivered an emotively blue version of 'Gloomy Sunday'. She felt into the words, bringing alive the notion of death's 'black coach of sorrow' confiscating the lover. She sang it in the voice she was going to use at the Fetish Club, when draped in a black boa she would extend a gloved arm to orchestrate the song's elegiac mood. And what Steve admired was her ability to live out the song, and to empathize so deeply with the lyrics that she appeared to be the song's solitary victim. She ceased to be the Lavinia he knew, and became someone invested with an aura of invincible power. Made fragile through vulnerability, she took refuge in the strength acquired through displaying the spectrum of grief that the lyrics required. Lavinia was so concentrated on her role that it was as though the room had ceased to exit, and she was on stage under a spotlight, the boards reddened with carnation heads thrown in homage to her dramatic rendition of smouldering ballads.

'We seem to have retrieved all of the missing sequins,' Lavinia commented, resuming her everyday expression, and divesting herself of the role she had carried to perfection.

'Now, shall I make you wait until I've sewn them all back on the dress? You can watch me while I sew, and think of your reward to come, when the dress is complete. How about that?'

Steve remonstrated that he couldn't hold out that long. He was uncomfortably large, and nerves were tingling at the base of his cock with the irritant persistence of columns of ants streaming after sugar grains. He knew that if she went down on him he would explode in the silk constriction of her mouth.

'I'll shoot a column to the ceiling five times, if I have to wait until you've sewn all those little sequins on the fabric,' he said, imploring her to grant him his reward. 'I want to keep the handcuffs on,' he urged, 'I'll be your captive. Let's do the 69 to start.'

He lay down flat, back to the carpet, while she, facing in the opposite direction, positioned her pussy above his mouth, arched her back, and brought her lips to the level of his cock.

'I can't take your panties down,' he said, 'I'm handcuffed.' They were both too urgent to debate the issue, and within seconds Steve was tonguing her slippery gusset, while she, sensing his climactic urgency, began by simply breathing on his cock, and then extending the exercise to prodding him intermittently with the tip of her tongue, a movement so slight that it carried the gentleness of a grassblade brushing the eyelid of someone asleep in the sunlight. It established an excruciating tickle in his cock. He could feel the insurgence of his orgasm building for detonative release. But Lavinia lingered as though she was blowing on hot food, and hadn't yet found the right temperature on which to bite.

He could feel her body arch and contract under his tongue, the successive orgasms rippling up and down the length of her spine. And being handcuffed excited him. He told her that there was a pink sequin got up her crack, and inserted his tongue into her vulva. She let out a sustained moan as he found the roots of her pleasure. She convulsed at his enquiring tongue, and without warning, swallowed his penis whole, taking it right to the back of her throat, and running her tongue along its underside. Steve relaxed and let go. The orgasm built like surf unfolding on a Pacific beach. It hung back in a white arc, crested, and then rushed forward with all the inexorable delivery of a wave.

They lay and rested for a while, before Lavinia sucked Steve alive again. 'You can have a second request,' she said, 'only my command is that you enter me.'

Her chameleonic adoption of moods had now afforded her the tone of a dominatrix. He waited like a slave over her body, while deliberating on what to ask.

'I want to make love to you while you're wearing your sequinned dress,' he said. 'And I'll help you resew all the sequins that get dislodged. If we go into the bed they can't escape the sheets.'

'But I've got to wear this dress next week at the Fetish Club,' Lavinia stressed. 'And I've told you that I can't sing without it. It's my private fetish.'

She deliberated for a while, and was clearly still sexually excited. 'All right,' she said. 'As a special favour, you can have me in the dress, but you really will have to pay the price of helping me sew the sequins back on. The trouble with the dress is it's old, and the stitching easily comes apart.'

Steve felt a glow of pleasurable apprehension as Lavinia wiggled across the room in her wet panties, and struggled into the dress. She put it on over her head, and for a moment, her hands up, and her prominent breasts showing, she looked like a pink flower, ascintillating tulip growing on the curved stem of a woman's body.

She came back to the bed, the hem rucked up around her waist, and Steve was urgent. He insisted that she release him from the handcuffs, as he wanted to feel her bottom full in his hands. He entered her with the authority of a master newly released from bonds. He went into her deep and had her cry out with pleasure. He impaled her with his expansive lust. She sobbed on the urgency of his feral rhythm. In his hands he felt the clusters of sequins, they were like a glitter-storm accompanying his lovemaking. He imagined how men viewing her on stage would desire her. They would imagine her naked, her pointed breasts blotched with crimson areolas, her bottom divided by a satin g-string. She would represent sultry mystique, a form of eroticism that was the more tempting for its inaccessibility.

As his excitement increased, so he had the desire to tear the sequins that clustered above her bottom. He felt like a mad grape-picker suddenly possessed by the desire to savagely rip black fruit off the vine. As they both neared simultaneous orgasm, so his nails scratched at the sequins like a cat. He could feel them being torn off and covering the bed. He lifted her bottom and brought it down on the sequins so they stuck to her buttocks. He fingered them into her anal crack, knowing he would have the task ahead of retrieving them. They exploded together like a summer storm, and lay collapsed in each other's arms, bodies crumpled into submission.

Steve knew the exhaustive task would begin all over again, but he was happy. He had joined himself to Lavinia as well as possessed the stage fetish which he knew would magnetize the audience on Wednesday night at the Fetish Club: Lavinia pooled under a single blue spotlight, singing 'Gloomy Sunday' in the bluest, heartbreaking tones.

Blues to Eat Your Heart Out

Jim felt no sense of psychological distress at his particular fetish, but he was anxious at times that it might interfere with his work as an assistant in an alternative record shop. Girls all the time were coming in dressed in the black PVC minis and leggings which fired his sexual mechanism. And particularly the goths with their post-punk accoutrements, girls in pink or red fun wigs or with spiky implants worked into their hair. Jim got turned on looking at their fish-net legs, their shiny black ankle-boots, and more often than not their PVC or leather minis. He spent a lot of time fantasizing about his fetishes, and was concerned to find a girlfriend who would dress according to his dictates.

In anticipation of this, Jim had taken to visiting Hyper Hyper and the Electric Ballroom, and had begun to acquire a personal collection of fetish garments. He devoted a wardrobe in his room to his private archive and painted it black outside and in, with silver stars liberally sprinkled across the paintwork. He bought metres of black PVC in Soho and lined the wardrobe shelves with this fabric. Part of his collection comprised catalogues of girls modelling PVC and leather, and the rest was garments. He liked skirts decorated with pronounced zips, particularly tight ones with the zip opening all the way down the front and back. And without a girlfriend to wear his personalized artefacts, he took to trying on the clothes himself, and the excitement this generated urged him into a nightly ritual of orgiastic self-gratification. He felt unsatisfied if he couldn't be alone with his fantasies for an hour each night, and this need became devotional; in time he found himself kneeling to an improvised altar of PVC boots, his lips tracing the outline of the toe and heel. He knew people who got off just by listening to Lou Reed's S&M narrative 'Venus in Furs', an old Velvet Underground track which had lost none of its sinister whiplash connotations. The reference to 'Shiny boots of leather' made a friend of his grow instantly hard, and this friend would make love to his girlfriend to the accompaniment of this song placed on endless repeat. It would trance them both out and heighten their orgasmic pitch.

Jim also liked the Velvet Underground and never tired of listening to their perverse drug and sado-sexual narratives, Lou Reed's cold unemotive expression serving to enhance the threat implied by the lyrics. So many Lou Reed enthusiasts came into the shop, as well as people into indie and techno-ambient music. Everyone had their own little cultic heroes, and defined their lifestyles through the music with which they associated. A lot of the PVC girls went for the last survivors of gothic like Siouxsie and the Banshees and Jesus and Mary Chain, and Jim liked to look at their make-up and see how they delineated their lips with a black pencil. He thought of them as a separate species, buttocks pronounced by black PVC hotpants, their concern with fetishistic detail causing excitement to travel all along his nerves.

Sometimes Jim would visit call girls and have them dress up in the PVC garments he owned, and cock firmly in his hand he would work himself off to the accommodating fantasy. He would have them teasingly unzip a shiny skirt before sitting on the bed, legs open, wearing nothing but PVC panties. He liked to savour the possibilities inherent in sex, rather than act them out, and he was anyhow in his own way waiting for the right girl. His mental perception of this girl was so intense that he was disappointed by almost everyone he met, for no one even approximated to his ideal. There were girls who had the right eyes, the right mouth, the right legs, the right bottom, and sometimes the right voice, but these were isolated characteristics, and nobody seemed to embody the perfect synthesis of all the qualities he required.

But at night he would return to his ritual. He placed a vase of red carnations above his altar of PVC boots, lit a subtle Japanese incense, put on music which heightened his erotic reveries, and then with shaking hands took out skirts and hotpants from his black wardrobe. He would then conjure to his mind the fetishistic image of the girl he wanted, and feel his cock expand to a hard resonant tissue. The act was becoming almost liturgical as the chords of 'Venus in Furs' reverberated through the room. Jim would jerk himself off in PVC gloves, the contact of the fabric in his penis, and the rhythm of shiny black fingers working up and down on his shaft bringing him to a devastating climax.

His work at the shop continued. Imports, re-mixes, picture sleeves, every sort of rarity passed through his hands, and he was responsible for pricing the stock. Aficionados of certain bands wanted everything. They combed through the latest additions three or four times a week, hungry to add to their collections and to have the latest news on new releases, fanzines, bootlegs, tours. Jim had a genuine interest in the whole infrastructure of collecting. He too hoarded his own scoop of Marc Almond and Scott Walker records, and would slip into a PVC jumpsuit to listen to the two great exponents of torch music.

It was a Saturday in autumn. London was turning Octoberish, and big yellow and orange leaves splashed the pavements and parks. Rain dazzled in intermittent showers. There was a feeling of the season exiting in a red ballroom gown. Jim took his lunch-hour break in Regent's Park and watched a variety of ducks punt their way across the lacquered ponds. He liked the Carolina species, with their exotic plumes. There was a solitary black swan dipping into the mirror surface.

Everything hung in stilled reflection. He liked to bring his melancholy to this place and drink in the scent of rotting leaves. He walked through an avenue of chestnut trees, his mind distracted by his sense of inner reflection. He didn't really know where he was headed, only that he was compelled to keep walking. Life was like that. You got into places and caught up with them later. Jim was deep in thought, and when he looked up he thought he was hallucinating.

There was a small shelter in front of him and in it sat a girl whose purple hair and PVC clothes immediately attracted him. It was like breaking direct into a dream. He could see her tiny PVC skirt and long fish-net legs; her eyes were green and her lips shocking scarlet. She had the ultra-feminine, locket-shaped face of which he had dreamt, and she was just staring at him as though he was late and she had been waiting her whole life for this fortuitous union.

'I've seen you in the shop,' she said quietly, and without reference to the fact they had never spoken before. 'I've been in a couple of times, although you've never served me.'

Jim couldn't believe this was really taking place. There was a sudden sparkle of rain as he stood in the entrance to the shelter, and to avoid getting wet he sat down on the bench beside her.

'I'm Melissa,' the girl said, recrossing her legs, and Jim watched the little strip of black plastic ride up her thighs. Melissa was a PVC fetishist's dream: her boots were made of the same fabric, and she wore a skimpy violet jumper under a black glossy top. Jim could see that she had pronounced breasts, and she spoke to him in the familiar confiding tones of someone he had known for a long time. The flurried rain sounded like it was shelling peas on the roof, and Jim was frightened he would blow his chances by failing to express the interest in her that his nerves registered.

'I'm sure working in that shop is only half of you,' Melissa said, and Jim felt like she had got into his head and was seeing him from the inside. 'You've probably got quite extreme tastes,' she continued. 'I once knew a boy like you, and he collected dolls, and he used to make them panties with his sewing-machine. When his parents left him money he bought a house and converted it into a doll's house, and he lived there with mannequins.'

'I'm not that bad,' Jim laughed, easing himself into possessing a voice, and with growing confidence he began to tell her a little about himself, and how for much of the time he felt himself in search of a purpose and somebody with whom to share his life. He lost consciousness of time and his job, and all the while he couldn't believe this meeting was taking place.

'I'm going to have to get back,' he told her, and then with impulsive passion he risked, 'Come to my place tonight at about eight. I'll get some wine, and I'll be expecting you.' He quickly wrote out his address on a scrap of paper, and without waiting for her response ran off into the autumn rain, crossing the orange park at a run, and out into the wet streets.

Jim felt agitated all afternoon. His mind was racing with the impossible realization that he had met the girl who conformed to his fetishistic ideals. He served customers in a trance. Someone wanted a Marc Almond Ectoplasmic Mix of 'The House Is Haunted', someone else a rare Tori Amos Japanese import, and there were requests for items by Syd Barrett, Julian Cope and The Grid. Jim mismanaged requests, and felt only the need to be alone, preoccupied with his thoughts of Melissa. Excitement was coursing through his veins and he had to restrain himself from outwardly showing his jubilance. In his mind he was imagining the elastic positions that Melissa would adopt under his guidance. He knew she would be wearing black PVC panties and that she would keep them on while he fucked her, and in the process heighten their mutual pleasure. He didn't know how he got through the afternoon, and it was still raining outside, for people came into the shop dripping with liquid diamonds.

He got away early, and picked up a couple of bottles of Mâcon Rouge at the Soho Wine Stores. The rain had eased off and he walked home at a sharp pace through the Soho streets.

Once indoors he proceeded to make himself up, applying black mascara and eyeliner. He slipped into a pair of PVC leggings, pulled on shiny knee-boots and awaited his visitor. He had lit candles above his altar of boots, and the room presented a gothic aura perfectly in keeping with its occupant. Jim liked headily resonant scents and sprayed a little Obsession into the air.

Melissa was prompt in her arrival, and Jim followed her up the stairs to his first-floor flat. His eye went directly up her seamed fish-net legs to the dangerously short hem of her PVC mini. The tautness in his groin was unbearable. He longed for her black-painted fingernails to tickle his cock out and for her dark red lips to swallow on his erection. He imagined he would shoot black pearls into her throat.

Melissa warmed to the tenebrous sexual atmosphere of Jim's flat. She sat back in an armchair, arranging her legs and attempting to retrieve her skirt from her hips. Jim felt it was like they had always known each other. Her lips came naturally to a heart-shaped pout, and her laugh vibrated with the promise of sensual pleasure.

'I can't believe we've just met,' Jim found himself saying. 'And if you'd come into the shop I would have fallen for you at once. It's more like you've stepped out of my head and into my life. I can't believe you're here.'

'Come and explore me then,' Melissa replied, and Jim was instantly fastening to her hot kiss, his hands working across her nipples, then down to make contact with the PVC skirt and boots. He thrilled on contact with the fabric. He knelt down and ran his tongue along her boots, up her fish-net thighs, and across her skirt. He savoured the taste of PVC, his fingers working at the fabric like a kitten's paws. When his fingers found her crotch he could feel it was outlined with silk. The contrast between the two fabrics excited him further. He extended the motion of his tongue to her pussy and drew from her sharp ecstatic moans. She was wet and in rhythm with his adventurous caresses. He folded her legs right over her shoulders in order to gain deeper access to her hot jewel. And when she twisted back up it was to bury her tongue in his throat and to tease his cock out with her black-painted fingernails.

It all happened just as he had imagined it, as though he was reliving a dream. Her lips closed over his penis at the base, and she began by running her tongue up and down his frenulum. It was an exquisitely teasing motion, and then she popped the cherry and swallowed all of him, positioning him for deep throat and running her tongue all over his alerted nerves. They built to a rhythm, but he wanted more. As he disengaged, so she slipped out of her fish-net tights and black silk panties, but sensing their mutual fetish, she kept on her PVC skirt, replaced her boots, and put on the PVC gloves which he offered her. Jim also responded to the ritual by dressing in a pair of PVC gloves and a top of the same fabric calculated to excite Melissa by its contact with her skin.

He heaped a great cache of shiny boots, skirts, and leggings on to the black counterpane, so that their lovemaking would involve all the symbols of their fetish. The adrenalin in his body was explosive. All of his fantasy objects were in evidence, and without any prompting on his part Melissa put on the crotchless PVC panties he had bought in anticipation of the right girl. He could see that she had streaked her pubic hair with dyes that were mauve, blue and green. She had a chain around her waist from which a miniature PVC boot was suspended. Jim kept on thinking that she couldn't be real, and that he was about to embrace his supreme sexual fantasy, rather than a woman. He delayed for fear of meeting with an illusion, but then she was drawing him down with a darting exploratory tongue, and fitting herself to the contours of his body. And without any effort he was swimming inside her, her gloved fingers hooking at his undulating flesh as their two bodies locked in a sensual geometry. They were both urgent, but restrained. Melissa moaned each time her body was covered by PVC garments, and Jim worked her back and bottom into the cool fabric. She arched her legs wider, and his black-gloved hands ran all over her body. Her glossy boots trailed up and down the backs of Jim's thighs, and then locked together round his waist. They were like a PVC python, and Jim built to a furious rhythm, his intensity increasing each time Melissa ran her gloved fingers over his bottom and balls. When they came together, her fierce cries reverberating through the flat, it was in a paroxysm of mutual fantasies.

And after making love a second time they lay together quietly, their need expended, their thoughts returning to the immediate, and outside they could hear the London rain tapping a slow drum-rhythm on the streets. Jim kept needing the reassurance that Melissa was real, and her best way of confirming this was to kiss him. But neither spoke about themselves; their private lives seemed unshareable, and each time Jim was about to ask Melissa about her life, and to enquire where she lived and what she did, he hesitated. And he seemed to have no desire himself to tell her of his personal history in the way that lovers impart fragmentary things which in time become a whole.

Eventually he fell asleep in Melissa's arms. When he awoke it was still raining, it was hardly dawn, but she had gone. The bed was in a chaos of fetish items. Jim lay there a long time. There was no note. Nothing. He began to think that he had dreamt Melissa, but when he sat up he saw the dark imprint of her lips on his stomach, a lipstick tattoo. It was the only trace of her, and he decided to keep the mark until that too should fade.